DIRTY DIAMONDS

DIRTY DIAMONDS

Betty Sullivan La Pierre

E-PUB2000

ISBN 1-59109-364-3

DIRTY DIAMONDS

To: Robert, Selma, Anne & Helen
Without you, I'd never have made it through this one.

CHAPTER ONE

Carl took Jamey by the shoulders and looked into her eyes. "Okay. It's almost time. Be ready to split the second I yell."

She shivered and slumped down on the edge of the hotel bed.

He pulled the truck keys from his pocket and placed them in her hand. "You'll do the driving. The cops won't be looking for a woman." He smiled as he leaned over and pecked her on the cheek. "Don't be scared, baby. Everything's going to be just fine."

Opening the tote bag she'd dropped on the end of the bed, he removed a suit coat and pre-knotted tie. Shrugging into the jacket, he slipped the tie over his head and let it hang loose around his neck, giving the appearance he'd just come in from a party.

Keeping his gaze on Jamey, he reached into his pocket and withdrew a pair of brass knuckles. She tapped the tips of her painted nails across her lips as she watched him shove them over his fingers.

He cuffed her lightly on the chin and grinned. "Yes, sweetheart, I know how to fight. When you're six foot two, you learn to use your brawn as well as your wit." He glanced around the room and snatched the cell phone off the bureau. Dropping it into the tote, he handed her the bag. "Bring this with you. Be sure we don't leave any evidence here."

Trembling she slipped the handles over her arm.

"Hey, what's the matter, sweetie, cat got your tongue?"

She shook her head. "No. Just a bit scared and nervous."

Pulling her toward him, he planted a long sexy kiss on

Jamey's lips, then held her at arms length and winked. "We'll celebrate when this is over. And if you think silk dresses and fake bangles around your wrist are pretty, just wait until you take a gander at the next ones we get."

Throwing a kiss, he nabbed the ice bucket from the bathroom and headed out the door. "Fix this so I can get in quickly," he said over his shoulder as he disappeared.

❧

Slipping the plastic 'Do Not Disturb' sign between the lock and facing, Jamey closed the door softly. She then dashed to the dresser and searched the drawers. Near the back of the bottom one, her hand closed around an item, which she whipped out and stuffed into her jeans pocket.

Within minutes, the shattering sound of gunshot caused her to bolt toward the entry. Carl staggered into the room, clutching his shoulder as blood soaked through his coat. Her heart pounded as he thrust two small velvet bags and the brass knuckles into her hands. "I'll be all right," he hissed. "Watch the newspapers. If all goes well, I'll meet you at Rusty's Bar in Amarillo in two weeks. Now get the hell out of here. Take the stairs." He gave her a shove toward the hallway before collapsing onto the floor.

Jamey dashed for the fire exit stairwell, raced down three floors, then charged out a side entrance. Frantic with fear, she kept looking behind her as she ran toward the front of the building. Stopping at the corner she caught her breath and glanced both ways, then walked swiftly down the sidewalk in the direction of where they'd parked the Tacoma. Just as she reached the black pick-up, she heard the wailing sirens in the distance. Her stomach tied in knots as she jumped inside the cab and locked the door. Throwing the brass knuckles into the tote, she shoved the two velvet bags into her purse and flipped on the ignition. Making a U-turn and keeping her eye on the mirrors, she bore down on the accelerator and headed toward the rear of the hotel. She held her breath until she knew for sure she hadn't been followed. Reaching one of the main streets, Jamey drove as fast as she dared.

When the apartment came into view, she sighed in relief and parked. She jumped out of the truck, dashed inside and secured the door behind her. Leaning against the wall, she took several deep breaths to regain her composure. "Stay calm," she said aloud. "Everything has gone as planned. Don't fall apart at the first stage."

Jamey went into the kitchen and sat down at the table. Her hands shook as she opened her purse and pulled out the pouches. Peering inside one of the bags, she moved it around until the light caught the glittering jewels. "Gorgeous," she gasped.

Glancing at the wall clock, she jumped up, realizing she couldn't risk staying here much longer. She crammed the small velvet sacks back into her purse, then went into the bedroom, snatched the already packed duffel bag from the closet and plopped it on the bed. Racing into the bathroom, she dampened a washcloth, then ran out to Carl's truck where she fiercely rubbed down the steering wheel, the stick shift, and any other surface she might have touched. Climbing out, she slammed the door shut with her butt.

Back inside the apartment, she picked up the duffel, whipped her purse straps over her shoulder and headed back out toward her own car. She tossed her luggage onto the passenger seat, then slipped behind the steering wheel. Careful of her speed, she made her way to west Interstate Forty. Her eyes narrowed as she stared down the road. "Goodbye sucker," she murmured.

Jamey Gray's stare was fixed on the freeway ahead, but her mind churned. Nothing must go wrong. Now, she'd be on her own for at least six months to a year before the final steps were completed.

Even though it brought tears to her eyes, the death of Aunt Rachel, her last relative on earth, couldn't have been more timely. She'd left Jamey with a small furnished cottage in Medford, Oregon, where she and Uncle Ross had lived for many years until he became ill. He wanted to spend his last days back in Oklahoma where he'd grown up, so they relocated and had rented the place for extra income. No one knew that Jamey's aunt and uncle had come from Medford, so it fit perfectly into her plans. That's where she would disappear for six months. She'd notified the renters that they had to move. But her first thoughts were how to lead Carl Hopkins off course, because she knew the minute they released him from the hospital, he'd come after her.

Carl had been chosen as the patsy because of his computer hacker abilities. She found him to be one of the most handsome nerds she'd ever met and he seemed equally intrigued with her, so the job of snaring him into a trap hadn't been difficult. However, she shuddered when she thought how it almost backfired the day he talked her into letting him move into her apartment. At first she'd objected, until he promised to pay the rent, utility bills and groceries, letting her use her pay check for personal purchases. It worked in the beginning, giving her more time to entice him with talk of diamonds and gems. Then he became possessive, which grated on her nerves. But things came to a climax last evening when he called her into the living room and pointed at the computer monitor.

"You see that?" he'd asked. "Those are Canadian diamonds."

She smiled when he kissed her arm and hooked his finger under the tennis bracelet dangling around her wrist. "All your talk about diamonds set me to thinking about this little bangle. These are only cubic zirconias. What if the stones in it were real?" He'd let out a whistle and flipped the bracelet, making it whirl around her arm. "That little baby would be worth a bundle."

She remembered gazing into his eager blue eyes and asking. "Why all the sudden interest in diamonds?"

He pointed at her. "It's your fault. You kept talking about all that beautiful jewelry in the shop where you work, plus the high prices of gold, diamonds and rubies. Those beautiful stones have to come from somewhere." He reached over and patted the computer. "So, I did research to find out how we could get some."

She pretended to scoff at his idea. "You're talking dangerous."

"It could be, but if we're careful, it should be a piece of cake."

She'd inadvertently told Carl about a diamond courier, Bob Evans, that her boss had talked about. For several months, Carl had tracked the man with his computer and cell phone. He'd discovered that the courier came to Oklahoma City about every three or four weeks with a briefcase full of diamonds to sell to local merchants.

"He carries enough diamonds to make four or five of those bracelets," Carl had told her in an excited voice.

When she warned him that some of the couriers carried guns, he waved off her concerns.

"This one's a real klutz," he said. "Stupid as they come. Doesn't even put the diamonds in the hotel vault. Instead, he takes them to his room." He then proceeded to tell her his plan.

Jamey remembered drifting into a natural high at his words, but the thought of jail time if they got caught, made her stomach quiver.

Shaking her head, she brought her thoughts back to the present and forced herself to focus on driving. This phase of the plan had ended successfully, so she could relax. She hoped to be rid of Carl Hopkins soon, so she wouldn't have to listen to any more of his rude remarks about her friends or his criticisms of her taste in clothes.

Next stop, Amarillo, Texas, where she'd begin phase two of her plan.

CHAPTER TWO

Exhausted and light-headed, Jamey finally reached the outskirts of Amarillo. Even though she'd stayed up all night many times before, the events of the last twenty-four hours had worn her out. She found a small, clean looking motel and checked in using her Visa card. Locking the door with the security chain, she showered, crawled into bed and fell asleep within minutes. Several hours later, she awoke refreshed.

She dressed in clean jeans and a tee shirt, then grabbed a small towel from the bathroom and spread it over the corner table. Adjusting the lamp to shine directly onto the surface, she fished out the two velvet bags from her purse and dumped the contents onto the cloth in two separate piles.

Jamey gazed at the glittering jewels for several minutes before she finally picked up one and rolled it between her fingers. Holding it up toward the light, she whispered. "Holy Shit! These suckers really sparkle."

She stashed the two carat stones back into their pouch and concentrated on the one carats still on the table. Removing her tennis bracelet from her wrist, she then fumbled through her handbag for the loupe and the small jewelry kit she'd lifted from work. Fortunately, she'd watched the jeweler repair loose stones in bracelets and rings by popping out the gems, then resetting them so they were tight. A valuable lesson.

She first adjusted the loupe to her eye and studied one of the stones. Placing that one aside, she picked up and viewed several more of the diamonds through the glass. "Damn, looks like they're all marked," she muttered.

Letting out a heavy sigh, she began her work. The job

proved to be tedious and slow as she had to be particularly careful not to snap off or weaken any of the prongs. Several times, she rubbed her eyes and stood to relieve her cramped back. Finally, after two hours, she finished extracting the thirty cubic zirconias from the bracelet. Then she rummaged through her jewelry case and found the extra velvet bag containing costume jewelry. She dumped the cheap stuff and dropped in the zirconias. Before dropping the last one into the bag, she held it up to the light alongside one of the stolen diamonds. She shook her head and surmised, that to tell the real from the fake, one would have to use a loupe.

Setting the real diamonds into the bracelet didn't take as long. Soon, she had the one carat stones snugly in place and closely examined her handiwork. Not bad for an amateur, she thought, fastening it to her wrist. Glancing at the many loose diamonds left on the table, she tried to count them, but her eyes were too tired. Goose bumps rose on her arms as she calculated the worth of all the gems she now had in her possession. In fact, it made her a bit nervous. Where could she safely put these jewels while she traveled across the country? It would have been better if she could have just hopped a plane, but that would also make her easier to find.

Pacing the room, Jamey knew she hadn't put enough thought into where to hide the diamonds until she actually held them in her hands. She glanced at the duffel bag, but shook her head. Not a good idea. She then picked up her purse, but dropped it. Too risky. "Where the hell's a good place?" she asked aloud.

Suddenly, she snapped her fingers and laughed. "Of course." Kneeling down beside her luggage, she dug out a brassiere, remembering that's where her grandmother had always carried cash or anything of value. She took out the sewing kit from her purse, removed the scissors and cut out the up-lift padding in the lower part of the bra. After stitching the velvet bags into each cup, she carried the undergarment into the bathroom where she pulled off her tee shirt and tried it on. She turned from side to side, studying her figure in the mirror, and decided she couldn't tell the difference. The pouches did the same job as the pads. This would work for now.

Not being as concerned about the zirconias, she stuck them into her jewelry case and tucked it into the duffel. Checking the bracelet around her wrist, she felt satisfied with her efforts. shoved the small pliers back into the kit and returned it to her purse. She took the map she'd purchased at the gas station, spread it out on the bed and rechecked the route, even though she'd memorized it. Calculating the miles in her head, she decided to call Tina Randolph in Los Angeles. They'd been best friends in high school and hadn't seen each other since graduation. Tina had left the day after they'd received their diplomas to take a job her aunt had promised in Los Angeles. The girls had kept in close contact, swearing they would get together soon. Tina would definitely be surprised to hear from her. Smiling to herself, Jamey folded the map and placed it in the side pocket of her purse.

She opened the drapes and stared out the window, figuring she'd better find an Oklahoma newspaper before traveling much farther. Maybe there would be some news about the jewelry heist and Carl's condition. If not, she could always go into the computer.

Gathering up her things, she wondered how long it would take before Carl realized she'd left. It probably depended on his hospital stay and if there were any police charges. Regardless, she figured there would be plenty of time to get cross country.

She closed her luggage, sat down on the edge of the bed and opened her wallet. Fingering the few remaining bills, she took a deep breath. The first thing she needed to do was hit an ATM.

Before leaving the room, she called Tina, who seemed ecstatic about their finally getting together. She gave Jamey detailed directions on how to get to her apartment and promised to leave a key under the doormat.

When Jamey hung up, her stomach growled, reminding her she hadn't eaten in many hours. While checking out, she asked the clerk to recommend a good restaurant and the location of the nearest bank or money machine. He directed her down the street where both were within walking distance of each other. When she entered the diner, she spotted the latest edition of "The Oklahoman" in the vending machine next to the door.

Scanning the headlines while waiting for her order, she didn't find anything about the robbery. There could be an article inside, so she'd have to scour the paper, page by page. Tucking it beside her, she ate her meal, then left in search of the bank. She found it easily and pulled the maximum amount allowed from the ATM. Checking the balance, she figured one more big hit would clean out that savings account. That should get her to California with cash to spare. She'd use Carl's gas card until the last minute.

Since she'd gotten a late start, the evening sun blazed through a bug smeared windshield, playing havoc with her view of the road, despite wearing sunglasses. She decided to stop early in the evening, get a few hours rest, then proceed the next morning with the sun at her back.

After two days of hard traveling, Jamey arrived in Los Angeles. She definitely didn't like what she saw. The air didn't smell fresh and too many vehicles cluttered the freeways. Thank goodness she didn't plan on staying in this area. A night's visit with Tina would be enough and then she'd head north.

Fortunately, her friend's apartment happened to be just off the freeway and Jamey located it without difficulty. She found the key under the mat as Tina promised and let herself inside. A welcome note awaited her on the coffee table. From the appearance of the furnishings, her friend had done well. However, Jamey noticed a man's clothes hanging in the closet of the bedroom where Tina had directed her to put her things. She'd never mentioned a husband or a lover. Jamey thought that odd, since she'd spoken openly of Carl.

She had time to freshen up and waited anxiously for Tina to get home from work. When she finally walked in the door, the two girls hugged and cried as if they were long lost sisters, both talking at once. Soon they settled down and gossiped deep into the night. Jamey told her friend about the diamond heist, but didn't divulge her involvement, only Carl's and how he'd been wounded and sent to the hospital.

Jamey's gaze went to the floor and her voice caught. "That's when I saw my opportunity to get out of the abusive relationship." She took a deep breath and forced a smile. "Enough about me. Tell me about what's been going on in your life all these years. Obviously, there's a man involved. His clothes are in the closet."

Tina squirmed in her chair. "He's been around ever since the job fell through that Aunt Sophie offered me out of high school. He found me a good place to work and got me this nice apartment. He comes by occasionally.

Jamey thought her evasiveness strange. Why didn't she call him by name? Maybe he's married. She decided not to probe as it seemed to make Tina uncomfortable, so she changed the subject.

"I think I'll go to Mexico for a few days. I need a rest." Jamey said, getting up and heading for the computer that sat on a table in the living room. "Can I use it?"

"Sure," Tina said.

Jamey booted up the machine and researched the airlines out of Los Angeles. "The prices aren't half bad, but they're still too rich for my blood."

Tina looked over her shoulder, biting her lip. "Oh man, I wish I could go with you."

Ignoring her remark, Jamey kept scrolling. "Think I better drive. I'll check "Maps" for the best route." She glanced at Tina. "You got any soda?"

"Sure, you want one?"

"Love it."

When her friend went into the kitchen, Jamey quickly pulled up the airline flights from Medford, Oregon, to Cancun, Mexico, to see if the prices had changed. She exited the site the minute Tina walked back into to the room. Going back to the map's site, she printed out the route to Mexico City.

Stepping away from the computer, she picked up the copy and sat down on the couch, pretending to study it. "This doesn't look like a difficult trip. Think that's where I'll head tomorrow."

"How long will you stay and where will you go after that?" Tina asked.

Jamey shrugged. "Not sure about either. But I promise to let you know where I settle."

The next morning, Jamey said her goodbyes and left.

Tina sadly watched her friend depart, then returned to her apartment with tears in her eyes. She sat down at the end of the couch and selected the picture of Jamey in her cap and gown from the corner table. Staring at it for several moments, she reminisced on how her life had never been as happy as when she and her best friend had shared so much fun in high school. However, she sensed that Jamey's life had been disappointing. When she spoke of Carl Hopkins her voice quivered and she seemed to withhold information. She'd read where women in abusive relationships felt guilty that they were somehow to blame for the treatment they received.

Of course, she'd lied too, and wondered if Jamey had picked up on her fabrications. But why burden her with the tales of her lover, Nick Albergetti, a con man always on the run, who thought he had to slap his women around a bit to show his superiority. Whenever the phone rang, she anticipated hearing he'd been thrown in jail or reported dead. Letting out a loud sigh, she replaced the picture and went into the kitchen where she took a soda from the refrigerator. She'd no more snapped off the top when the front door burst open.

"Hello, sweetheart. Your Nick is home."

She smiled and had to admit he was the most handsome thing she'd ever seen. Tall, dark and handsome, no other way to describe him. But he could be mean, so she reluctantly flung her arms around his neck and hugged him close.

"What are you doing home from work? Are you sick?" he asked, holding her at arm's length and studying her face with a grim expression. "Were you expecting someone?" His hands gripped her wrist.

She struggled to get her arms away. "Nick, let go, you're hurting me."

"Is there another man?"

"No, of course not," she said, disgustedly. "I just saw my girlfriend off. The one from high school, Jamey Gray. Remember, I told you she was heading this way?"

He released his hold and smiled. "Oh, yes. That's right, I forgot. The one fleeing Oklahoma and leaving her boyfriend. What's his name?"

"Carl Hopkins."

He went to the refrigerator and popped open a beer. "Did she tell you the reason she left him?"

Tina rubbed her wrists as she told him the story about the diamond heist, but omitted the word 'abuse' from the tale. He listened with interest.

"So where's she going?"

"Right now, she's headed for Mexico, but I don't know where she'll go after that. I made her promise to call me the minute she found a place to live."

Later, he noticed the light on the computer and brought it up out of its sleep mode. Clicking on the last places visited, he scrolled down and spotted an airline inquiry. He went to the location and it asked if he'd like to go back to the previous entry. Clicking okay, he studied with curiosity the listing of departures from Medford, Oregon, to Cancun, Mexico. But not thinking too much about it, he shut down the computer.

ஃ

Jamey had found out from Tina the location of the nearest ATM machine and withdrew the remaining money in her account. Okay, that's the end of Jamey Gray's savings, she thought, placing the bills in a zippered compartment in her wallet. She then drove into a gas station and used the gas card for the last time. Staring at the pieces of plastic in her hand, she knew Carl would track the electronic trail to Los Angeles, which would no doubt lead him to call on Tina. As much as she loved her friend, she knew the girl couldn't keep a secret if her life depended on it. Therefore the Mexico story should lead Carl off track, if he called any day soon.

After filling the tank, Jamey pulled off to the side of the building and took the little Swiss Army knife that she carried in her purse, flipped out the tiny scissors and cut up the credit cards. Next she removed a small bundle from the duffel bag and took out her new Visa cards and driver's license. She compared the fake one with the name Jasmine Louise Schyler to the original and marveled at how real it looked. Using the Schylers' name was her idea, even though it might not have been the wisest choice. They were good people and she missed them.

Sighing, she stuck the old Jasmine Louise Gray license into her luggage, just in case she needed it somewhere down the line, and slid the new one into her wallet. Gathering up the plastic pieces, she went into the lady's room and tossed them into the trash can.

Jamey's real name was Jasmine Louise Gray. Her parents were killed in an automobile accident the day after she turned twelve. She was an only child and her Aunt Rachel had always felt bad that she couldn't take Jamey. But at the time of the accident, she had a very ill husband and it drained all her energy just to care for him. The Schylers, who had been friends of the family for years, felt pity and took Jamey into their home.

But life had been hard during her youth. When Jamey turned sixteen, her foster mother had to be put into a home for Alzheimer's disease and passed away within a few months. Then shortly after her eighteenth birthday, her foster father died. Although the Schylers had struggled all their lives, they left Jamey with a small inheritance which she'd stashed away under the name of Jasmine Louise Schyler. She hoped it would carry her through until the plan could be carried out. Jamey never told Carl anything about the Schylers and she doubted Tina even remembered their name as they never attended any of the girls' school activities.

She didn't plan to notify her landlord back in Oklahoma, nor would she fill out any change of address at the post office when she applied for her box number. As far as bill collectors were concerned, Jamey Gray had vanished.

Climbing into the car, she wondered how long she'd be stuck in Medford. Her money would hold out for a couple of months, but then she'd have to sell some of the diamonds to survive. That's when she'd have to be very careful of her timing. Driving out of the station, she turned onto the ramp labeled 'North Interstate Five'.

CHAPTER THREE

Jamey Schyler arrived in Medford, Oregon before dark, found the small cottage without any problem and immediately fell in love with the location. It sat in the middle of an open field with no nearby neighbors. The outside needed paint and it had no lawn, but she didn't care as long as there was running water, heat and privacy.

She let herself in the front door and flipped on the light, relieved to see the utilities had not been turned off. Exploring the rest of the house, she discovered the back door stood slightly ajar. On closer examination, she found the locking mechanism taped in such a fashion that it could be pushed open or shut without a key. The chain guard remained intact, so she removed the tape and found the lock still worked. That explained the roach clips and burned down candles she'd noted in the different rooms. She figured the local teenagers had discovered the vacant house and made it their hide out. Their playtime would come to a screeching halt now that she'd arrived.

Fortunately, the dust covers draping the furniture of this fully furnished house were still in place and nothing appeared damaged. Jamey picked the biggest bedroom of the two and put away her scant possessions, then found a vacuum cleaner in the hall closet. By dusk, she had things in pretty good shape. Trekking back and forth to the car, she realized the back entry seemed more convenient and would be the one most used. So she threw the dead bolt on the front door and slid the big overstuffed chair in front of it. The relocation of the piece of furniture made the living room appear much larger.

She'd just pulled the last of the dust covers off the furniture and dropped them into a pile to launder when she heard the knock. Warily, she peeked around the corner toward the living room and caught her breath. She could see the silhouette of a tall man through the sheer drape covering the glass panel on the front door.

"Who's there?" she called.

"My name's Tom Casey. I'm a private investigator. May I speak with you."

Jamey's stomach lurched. Would Carl have hired a private eye? She pushed the thought from her mind. How would he know where I am? Keep your cool, she cautioned herself. Find out what the man wants before you panic. "Could you come around to the back, please," she called.

She watched the figure move off the porch, then positioned herself at the back door with a hand on the knob, her body blocking the entry. When he approached, her gaze traveled from his feet upward. The cowboy boots and jeans reminded her of a ranch hand. But when she saw the black eye patch, she stepped back and gripped the door handle. "Uh, yes. What do you want?"

"Sorry, didn't mean to startle you. But I've been keeping a watch over this place since the renters left. When I saw your car and the lights on, thought I'd better check it out."

She eyed him suspiciously. "Well, if you're a private investigator, you haven't done a very good job. This place has been used as a hide out for a bunch of pot smoking kids."

He raised his brows. "You're serious?"

"I certainly am. Here's the evidence." She held a paper sack toward him. "Just look at all these roach clips and burned candles I found in every room."

"I see," he said, peering into the bag.

She dropped the sack onto the floor and put a hand on her hip. "I don't think my Aunt Rachel would be too happy about this."

"Is that Rachel Smith?"

Jamey nodded and sighed. "Yes, my aunt. She passed away

a month ago back in Oklahoma. Since I'm the sole survivor, I inherited this house. I'm surprised you weren't notified."

"No reason to. I'm not on a payroll or anything. Just did it as a favor. I'm sorry to hear the news. I knew the Smiths when they lived here. Fine people." He hooked his thumbs in his front pockets. "What's your name?"

"Jasmine Louise Schyler. Would you like to see some identification?"

"No, that's not necessary, Ms. Schyler. I won't keep you from your chore of moving in." He turned to leave then stopped. "By the way, have you recorded the deed at the court house yet?"

"No, but I will, thank you."

He handed her one of his business cards. "Welcome to Medford and if you need any help, just give me a call at this number."

❧

After two weeks of not leaving the small cottage other than for a few errands, Jamey felt like the walls were closing in on her. The television left in the house worked, but she found herself flipping through the channels when nothing caught her interest. Never a couch potato, she didn't plan on starting now. She knew she had to keep a low profile, but could she stand six months of this boredom?

A stray kitten had wandered up to her house shortly after she'd moved in and refused to leave. Jamey finally let the cat inside and named her Mitzi. The animal had been entertaining and taken away part of Jamey's loneliness, but didn't fill a twenty three year old girl's need for people. There must be some place where she could meet men and women her own age without taking too much of a risk.

She'd met Ellen, a single gal, at the laundromat, but she worked full time and sometimes late into the evening, seldom free to go anywhere. The rest who frequented the laundry, were all married women with kids. She grew tired of hearing the antics of their husbands and children.

However, Ellen informed her that the most popular place in town was Curly's Bar & Grill. It had a live band on the weekends, a dance floor and good food to boot. Sounded like her kind of place. Ellen promised to take her tonight since she didn't have to work Saturday. Jamey could hardly wait and had already selected a silk dress to wear.

She stood staring out the window at her ten year old Celica with its dents and fading paint. The gems were safely tucked behind the ashtrays and under the seats. No one would want that ugly hunk of junk. Even the local teenagers would be embarrassed to steal it and take a joy ride. She didn't think it a good idea to leave the jewels in the house, especially since she'd already had some trouble with kids in the area. They persisted in shouting crude remarks and throwing rocks at the place as they walked by. She figured they might get real bold one day and try to break in when she wasn't home. If the harassing didn't subside soon, she'd have to call the cops, but would delay as long as possible.

To help pass the time before meeting Ellen at Curly's, Jamey propped Carl's laptop that she'd taken from the apartment, onto her knees and searched the Oklahoma papers' websites. She had done this every day in hopes of finding any updated newspaper articles on the robbery. The only ones she'd found described a struggle in the hotel room between the diamond courier, Bob Evans, and Carl Hopkins. Evans had suffered a broken jaw and Hopkins had received a non-life threatening gunshot wound. Carl had denied stealing anything from Evans, claiming he'd inadvertently gone to the wrong door after getting ice. Evans had attacked him, wielding a gun, and Hopkins had fought for his life. During the struggle the gun discharged hitting him in the left shoulder. Authorities had found an ice bucket and water stains near the door which made them believe his story. The police had searched Hopkins' person and the hotel room, but none of the missing gems were found. A hearing was set for the following week.

Jamey had found only one other news article that appeared after the hearing. The company responsible for the lost diamonds decided not to press charges against Hopkins, who was still in the hospital and wouldn't be released for several more days. There was no mention of any accusations against the courier.

It had been over a week since that last article and she doubted there would be any more. Well, Carl had told her to watch the papers. Too bad he didn't show up in Amarillo, she thought, smiling to herself. Such a shame to leave me with all these beautiful stones.

Hugging Mitzi close to her chest, Jamey's smile quickly vanished when she realized that once Carl went to the apartment and discovered she'd absconded with the diamonds, all hell would break loose. With his computer skills, he'd track her to Los Angeles, and she prayed he'd lose her trail and give up.

Jamey quickly went into Carl's credit card accounts and checked his latest billings. So far there had been none, so she assumed he hadn't left Oklahoma yet. She knew Carl wouldn't give up on finding her and the tale she'd told Tina about her going to Mexico to lead him astray probably wouldn't work now, too much time had lapsed since she'd left Los Angeles.

More than likely he'd bug Tina to find out if she knew anything. Fortunately, Tina knew nothing and Jamey certainly didn't intend on calling and telling her where she ended up. But, she didn't dare let her guard down and underestimate Carl's ability at the computer. As careful as she might be, he'd find some way to trace her. So, how long did she have before he eventually followed her to Medford?

CHAPTER FOUR

Jamey, not wanting anything to spoil her time at Curly's tonight, pushed the thoughts of Carl from her mind. She started to put the computer away, but on second thought decided she'd better send an e-mail. Typing in the address, she put nothing but her new phone number in the subject area and sent it off. Then she tucked the computer into the closet corner and jumped into the shower.

Anticipating tonight, she spent extra time in front of the mirror on her hair and make-up. She felt like a high school girl attending her first prom. It had been a long time since she'd actually gone out and partied.

The girls had agreed to drive their own cars and meet at Curly's when the action began, usually around nine o'clock. Jamey lucked out and found a parking spot in front. Many heads turned her way as she entered the establishment and walked across the floor to Ellen's booth.

∾⋖⋗∾

Mark Spencer stood behind the bar and gave out at a low whistle when Jamey came in the door, her pale green silk dress clinging to her curves and the color accenting her shiny blond hair. He nudged his dad. "Who's that?"

Curly slipped on his glasses and squinted toward Jamey. "Never seen her before. Wonder if she needs a job?"

Mark grinned and shook his head as he filled a glass. "Dad, you never cease to amaze me."

"Hey, I need another waitress. And that gal's a looker. What did those two girls just order?"

"Gin and tonic."

"Hand me the tray."

Curly sauntered over to the booth. "Welcome, ladies, don't think I've ever seen you in my place before. Are you visiting our area?"

Ellen spoke first. "Hi, I'm Ellen. I've been here about six months. This is the first time I've actually had a whole weekend off work. It's good to be out."

"Welcome. Too bad you've already got a job. I could sure use some extra girls." He set the drinks in front of them. "Your first drink is on the house."

"Wow, thanks."

He smiled at Jamey and lifted his brows. "And who are you?"

"I'm Jamey. I've only been here a few weeks."

"You working?"

"No."

"If you need a job, just come and see old Curly. I'll guarantee you good wages, not to mention tips, and a fun place to work. Have a good time and hope you come back again soon." He smiled and nodded, then went back to the bar.

A drum roll brought everyone's attention to the band and the floor filled. Jamey danced every song. Even Mark took a break and led her onto the floor.

"I'm Mark Spencer, Curly's son. You new in town?"

"Yes, I've only been here a short while."

"What's your name?"

"Call me Jamey." Then she glanced toward the bar. "Was your dad serious when he said he's hiring?"

"Yeah, one of his cocktail waitresses got married last week, so he's short of help. Why? You interested?"

"Not sure. But I'll think about it."

That night in bed, Jamey, with Mitzi snuggled against her back, thought about the wonderful time she'd just spent with her own peers. A job at Curly's would definitely take the monotony out of her life, but exposing herself to the public could be dangerous and risky. Did she want to take that chance?

She slept restlessly and awoke early. Slipping on her robe, she sat at the kitchen table, sipping a cup of coffee and thought about Curly's job offer. She'd had experience as a cocktail waitress and was damned good at it, not to mention she liked it. If he didn't require a lot of paperwork to hire her and she could pick her hours, it just might work out. Her best bet would be to work the later shift, when the young people were there. They didn't keep up on the news like the older crowd. She doubted the story about the Oklahoma diamond heist would ever reach Oregon, but she couldn't be sure. One of the news articles did state a woman had accompanied Carl to his room. Fortunately, it didn't carry a description or indicate that she might be involved.

Drumming her fingernails on the kitchen table, she stared into space. Mitzi scrambled onto her lap and started chasing her hand. Jamey laughed and swooped her into her arms. "You silly cat. You're so cute. But you can't get on the table." Cuddling the animal in her lap, she rubbed its ears. "After I get the phone call later today, I'll be able to make up my mind. If all goes well, Mitzi, you'll have to be a good girl while I'm at work." She deposited the cat onto the floor and went to get dressed.

Later that afternoon, she waited anxiously by the phone. Finally it rang and she grabbed the receiver. "Hello."

"I'll make this snappy. Everything's delayed. Count on double the time there."

"What if I get a job?" Jamey asked.

"Okay. But watch your back. I'll call in two weeks."

The line went dead.

Jamey hung up and put a small star on her calendar marking the time for the next call. Then she decided to run over and talk to Curly before the bar opened.

Three weeks after Jamey's visit, Tina received a message from Carl Hopkins on her answering machine. She didn't return the call due to Jamey's warnings. However, when he finally reached her in person, Tina succumbed to the man's mournful voice explaining he wanted Jamey back and how much he loved her.

When Tina related Carl's conversation to Nick, his curiosity grew. He questioned her about Jamey's whereabouts, trying to keep it in an off handed manner as not to arouse her suspicions. To him, it just didn't fit that some gal would leave her guy after a diamond heist. When he spotted the Medford, Oregon, to Cancun, Mexico inquiry on the computer, he didn't think much about it then, but now it made sense. He knew that if Tina had any idea of where Jamey had gone, she'd have told him and Carl.

The next morning, Nick waited until Tina left for work before logging onto the internet. He went into National Newspapers, clicked on 'The Oklahoman" and put Carl Hopkin's name into the archives. It didn't take long before the first article popped up telling about Hopkins' confrontation with a well-known diamond courier, Bob Evans. The tone of the news article left Nick guessing at how much these diamonds might be worth. But from the wording, he figured they must be quite valuable. He knew about gems. The insurance companies were keeping it quiet for a reason. They probably wanted to find the jewel thief through networking in hopes of getting the jewels back before they involved the police or FBI.

Since no diamonds were found on Hopkins or in his room, Nick wondered if this courier had pulled a fast one. Then he found the article where one sentence jumped out at him. 'The clerk at the hotel said a woman had accompanied Hopkins when he checked in.'

That's all Nick needed to see. He put two and two together real fast. Ms. Jamey Gray had absconded with the diamonds. And no way in hell had she taken off for Mexico with them. Knowing Tina couldn't keep a secret, her friend had fed her a story hoping she'd pass it on to Hopkins, giving Jamey time to get out of the area. However, too much time had passed now.

He shut down the computer, strolled over to the corner

table that Tina kept filled with pictures and picked up the photo of Jamey. Having never met the woman, he studied it for several minutes, storing her features into his memory. Nick had a sneaky suspicion that this wasn't a one person operation, that it had been planned for some time. How long would she remain in Medford? She obviously planned on meeting someone in Cancun in the near future. But when?

He pulled out the picture and slipped it into his jacket pocket. If Jamey didn't use her real name, the photo, even though a few years old, would come in handy. Not wanting to put the empty frame back on the table, he shoved it onto the shelf in the top of the cloak closet.

Figuring he only had a certain amount of time before Jamey disappeared completely, he called Tina at work, "Hello, my little sweetheart. Got some bad news. I've just been called out on a job, so I won't be seeing you for about a week, maybe even longer. I'll miss you too. Be good and keep the bed warm."

It would have been faster for him to fly, but he didn't dare take the chance with all the new regulations. Being an ex-felon, packing a gun in his luggage would prove risky.

The long eleven hour drive would give him time to formulate some sort of plan to find Jamey Gray. He'd checked Medford, Oregon on the internet and discovered the population to be approximately sixty thousand. Not a big place, which would make it a lot easier to hunt her down.

Jamey was a good looking woman with no formal education. If she needed work quickly, she'd likely apply for a job as a restaurant or cocktail waitress where turnovers happened on a regular basis. He remembered Tina telling him about Jamey doing this type of work and some of the funny stories she'd told. He'd start with the bars and ask around about the popular hang outs.

But questions kept popping into his mind. Why would she need to work if she had a load of diamonds? She could find a fence, hock some or just lay low. Why, of all places would she go to Medford, Oregon? Did she know someone there? Tina had told him that Jamey was an only child and her parents had died before she reached high school age. Tina couldn't remember the names of the people who took Jamey into their home. Surely, if there had been relatives in Oregon, Jamey would have ended up in that neck of the woods.

He just might find himself on a wild goose chase. He felt the corners of his mouth twitch. It wouldn't be the first time. But usually his hunches were right on. For whatever reason, he'd soon learn why this girl went to Medford, Oregon.

Within an hour, Nick Albergetti was heading north on Interstate Five.

CHAPTER FIVE

Nick made good time and arrived at the outskirts of Medford by ten o'clock that night. He found a motel and went to bed, figuring he'd start his search first thing the next morning.

By afternoon of the next day, he'd accumulated enough information to start bar hopping that night. Curly's Bar & Grill had the most points on Nick's list for sporting the best looking cocktail waitresses in town. He'd shown the photograph of Jamey at several gas stations and a couple of the attendants said she resembled the new gal working at Curly's.

That pretty well confirmed his hunch. Tonight he'd see for himself. He drove past the bar a couple of times and noted the sign out front advertising a live band on the weekends. Perfect, he thought. It's Saturday and the place will be hopping.

Jamey shouldn't recognize him, if he'd made a believer out of Tina. He'd threatened her some time ago that it could cost him his life if she ever told anyone his name or displayed a picture. It took a good roughing up and destroying a couple of digital cameras before she finally understood he meant business. However, he speculated, here were two girlfriends from high school who'd finally gotten together after many years. Some of his clothes hung in the guest room closet of Tina's apartment. Jamey would naturally be curious and ask questions. Tina swore she hadn't told her girlfriend anything about him, but he knew his woman. She'd lied to him before and had a hard time keeping her mouth shut. Jamey might have pulled out a description of him or even a first name. He'd just have to play it cool and watch for any tell tale signs of recognition.

Jamey loved her job at Curly's. It hummed with customers and she liked keeping busy. She'd just run back to the ladies' room to take a breather and freshen her lipstick when one of the other waitresses dashed in to do the same.

"Oh, Jamey, did you see that gorgeous hunk of a man that just came in?"

She shook her head. "No. But, I'll sure check him out when I go back inside."

"He's gorgeous. Looks Italian. Never seen him before. He's sitting in your station area at the far booth. Yummy. Times like this I wish I didn't have a boyfriend." She winked and hastened back toward the bar.

Jamey felt that familiar chill slide down her spine and wondered if she should heed the warning. She slowly walked to the curtained doorway and peeked out toward the corner booth. Susy had it right; he definitely was a handsome brute. But any strange face made her nervous. Straightening her uniform, she cut through toward the bar and picked up a tray. She made her way toward the newcomer, collecting empty glasses and taking orders as she went.

"Good evening, sir. What can I get for you?"

Nick glanced up from reading the menu. His brown eyes twinkled as they reflected the glow of the lit candle in the middle of the table. "Uh, yes. I'll have an order of the hot wings along with a Scotch and water."

"Very good," Jamey said, tucking the menu back in the holder. "Be back in just a few minutes."

She felt his stare boring into her back as she left the table. Soon, she returned with his drink and went about her business taking care of other customers. Jamey sensed his gaze following her from table to table. Her hand trembled as she served other clients. Attractive men usually didn't bother her and she enjoyed their attention. So, why did this man make her so nervous? He hadn't flirted or made any advances, only given his order. She decided that penetrating glare is what made her uncomfortable.

When she delivered his hot wings order, he grasped

her wrist before she moved away. "You are quite a beautiful woman."

A blush burned her cheeks. "Thank you."

"I see from your name tag, you're Jamey." He glanced at her hand. "And there's no ring on your finger. Could it be my good fortune that you're unattached?"

"I'm sorry, sir, I'm not supposed to socialize with the customers. Please excuse me, I have to get back to work."

Jamey turned away, feeling butterflies flit through her stomach. She certainly wouldn't mind talking with him more, but didn't want to risk Curly or Mark spotting her spending too much time at his table. And Mark had already indicated he liked her.

After about an hour, Jamey noticed the stranger moving toward the cash register to pay his bill. He then headed toward her and tucked a hefty tip into her apron pocket. Smiling, he winked and said, "Maybe I'll see you soon."

"Thank you, Mr....?"

"Call me, Nick."

The other waitresses teased her about always alluring the best looking men. Laughing it off, she went about her duties. These guys came and went. She'd probably never see him again. At closing time, she turned in her apron and headed for the back door toward the alley where the employees parked.

About half-way home, she glanced in the rear view mirror and noticed a car about a half a block behind her. At first she didn't pay much attention, until the vehicle kept making the same turns she did. Surely this wouldn't be the good-looking guy that came into the bar tonight. He seemed more sophisticated than that.

Her heart pounding, she kept her eye on the mirror as she approached the cottage. The car still followed. Not wanting to lead him to her house, she headed back to work and breathed a sigh of relief when she saw Curly's car still parked in front. She ran to the front door yelling, "Curly!" Curly!"

When he finally answered her frantic pounding, he pulled her inside. "What the hell's the matter? You look like you've seen a ghost."

Almost at the brink of tears, Jamey explained what had happened. "I didn't want him to see where I lived, so I came back here, praying you hadn't left."

"You did the right thing." Curly said. "I'll go out and check."

In a few minutes he returned. "There's no one out there. You probably just imagined it. It's a bit spooky this late at night for a woman to be out alone. So, hold on just a second and let me finish cleaning up. I'll follow you home and make sure you get there safe and sound."

He stayed close behind her until she pulled up to the cottage. And he didn't leave until she got inside and signaled him by flipping the porch light off and on.

Her heart still pounding against her rib cage, she went from room to room and checked to make sure all the windows and doors were shut and secured. She sat in the dark for a few minutes watching the road, then sucked in her breath when she spotted a car slowly driving down the street without lights. It acted like it was going to stop in front of her place just as another car turned the corner. Never did she think she'd be glad to see a cop cruising until that moment. The black and white stopped beside the other car and shined a flashlight beam at the driver. Jamey couldn't see the man's face, but could tell he shrugged his shoulders. She heard the car roar as if he'd accelerated in the wrong gear. Then, the person inside waved at the policeman, flipped on his lights and drove off.

She shivered as she witnessed this event, then groped her way back to her bedroom in the dark. Taking her pistol from the closet shelf, she slipped it under her pillow, kicked off her shoes, then wiggled under the covers fully dressed. Mitzi jumped up on the bed and snuggled close.

After a restless night, Jamey got up early and padded from window to window searching the area and street for any unusual vehicles or people. When nothing appeared out of the ordinary, she breathed a sigh of relief. Last night had really shaken her. Maybe she needed protection; her life could be at stake. She didn't classify herself a sissy, but she feared being tortured into revealing where the gems were hidden. And if she did hire an investigator, what kind of a story could she make up that would convince him to take the case. She definitely couldn't tell the truth.

But who? She snapped her fingers and dug into her purse for the business card the guy with the eye-patch had given her when she first moved in. When she finally found it, she sat down and sipped a cup of coffee as she read his information. 'Tom Casey, Private Investigator' was printed above the address and phone number.

Hawkman's one room office in Medford had the disadvantage of being situated over a donut shop, and the scent of freshly baked pastries swirled around his nose. Propping his feet on the desk, he attempted to concentrate on bringing his books up to date, but shook his head as he tried not to think about those delicacies that had already taken their toll on his waistline. Jennifer, his wife, had pointed this out by pinching the love handles forming around his middle.

Out of the corner of his eye, he caught the motion of the door slowly opening. He dropped his feet to the floor and placed the ledger on the desk. He watched in silence as a hand with long red fingernails wrapped around the door's metal edge and shoved it open a few more inches. A youthful face framed by long blond hair poked through the crack. Big brown eyes peeked out from underneath straight bangs.

"Hi there, Mr. Tom Casey, private eye."

Hawkman came to his feet. "Ms. Jasmine Schyler. Come in."

She surveyed the room before stepping inside, then closed the door. Hawkman motioned toward the chair in front of his desk. "Have a seat." He observed that her face looked different from the first night he'd met her. She didn't look as pretty. Maybe because now she'd drawn on thick eyebrows and outlined her mouth over the lip line with bright red. Her skin tight jeans, along with the cropped top that didn't meet the waist band, revealed her slender figure. A gold belly-button ring completed the picture.

She plopped into the chair. Hawkman studied the young woman for a few moments, noticing the dark circles under her eyes.

"You look down right pooped."

"I didn't get much sleep last night."

He noticed a tinge of fear flicker in her eyes as her gaze dropped to the surface of his desk. "Why?"

"Someone followed me home from work. I got so scared I went back to the bar and got Curly."

Hawkman leaned back in his chair. "Curly Spencer?"

"Yes." She forced a smile. "I work at his place now and like it a lot."

"Curly's a good man. Did he catch anyone that looked suspicious?"

She shook her head. "No. He followed me home and made sure I got inside safely. But I couldn't sleep, so I watched out the living room window for a couple of hours."

"And did you see anything?"

"Yes. A car with no lights drove down my street and almost stopped until a cop just happened to cruise by. The person faked car trouble and drove off." She glanced up. "I'm here to hire you as my body guard."

Hawkman waved off her suggestion. "Probably just some jerk from the bar wanting a date with a good looking woman."

The corners of her mouth twitched. "Wish I could believe that, but I think an old boyfriend is out to get me."

He came forward, placing his arms on the desk. "Why's that?"

Clutching the small handbag close to her body, she stared at him. "Because I up and left him without a word. I got tired of his abusive behavior. He scares me to death." She squirmed in her seat. "I can give you five hundred dollars right up front, if you'll protect me."

Hawkman pulled a yellow legal pad in front of him. "Tell me a little history and we'll go from there." Picking up a pencil, he began to write. "Let's see, if I remember right, your full name is Jasmine Louise Schyler."

"Yeah, but I can't stand my name. Everyone just calls me Jamey."

"That's fine," he said, jotting down her name with (Jamey) in parenthesis and her address which he knew. "What's your phone number?" As he wrote, he wondered where this woman could get five hundred dollars to pay him up front. She'd just started working. He did notice the flashy tennis bracelet dangling from her wrist and decided she had access to money from somewhere. He leaned back, crossed an ankle over his knee and tapped the pencil on his cowboy boot. "Okay, Ms. Schyler, you're saying you want twenty-four hours a day protection service? That's pretty expensive."

She put a finger to her lips. "What I want you to do is make sure this guy stays away from me."

"I have no idea who you're talking about. Is it the man you think followed you or the old boyfriend?"

"I'm not sure they aren't connected."

"Okay, then start from the beginning and tell me why you think someone is after you."

Jamey took a deep breath. "It all started back in Oklahoma."

Hawkman raised a brow.

Her eyes slightly narrowed. "Well, what's so odd about that?"

"I didn't say a thing."

"You didn't need to. Your expression showed it."

"Sorry, didn't mean to mislead you, but, you're in Oregon now. Does this boyfriend know you're here?"

"No."

"Did you tell him about your inheritance?"

"No."

"Do you owe him money? Or did you take something of his?"

"No."

"Don't you think you're being a little paranoid? How can a

guy chase down his girlfriend if he has no idea which direction she went." He dropped his pencil on the desk. "You know, there are a lot of shy guys around here who might follow a pretty woman, but never approach her. Did you get a good look at the person in the car?"

She shook her head. "No."

"So, you're just making the assumption that your ex-boyfriend hired a guy to do you harm?"

Jamey shrugged. "Yeah, I suppose."

"Give me some specifics so I can decide if this case is worth pursuing. Otherwise, you'll have to find somebody else."

She jerked up her head and slapped a hand on the desk surface. "I don't want anyone else. I heard you're the best."

"Thank you. Appreciate that." He picked up the pencil and began writing on the pad. "Everything you tell me is confidential unless it's against the law. So let's get started." He pulled a form from the top desk drawer. "You say you're working at Curly's Bar & Grill?"

She nodded. "Yes."

He glanced up and smiled. "I've known Curly and Mark for a long time."

She grinned and appeared to relax. "Mark's cute."

"Has he gone into business with his dad?"

No. He goes to college and is gone most of the day. He only helps out on Friday and Saturday nights."

"Is he your new beau?"

"Well, sort of, but not a steady yet," she said, shrugging.

"You know if the word gets out that you're Mark's girlfriend, the guys won't bother you. So, why don't you give things a little more time and see if you're followed again?"

Her features tightened and a scowl formed on her lips. "Because, except for my cat, I'm alone. And I'm frightened. Especially after getting up this morning and finding this note poked inside my screen door." She pulled an envelope from her purse and handed it across the desk. "He must have somehow followed Curly and me last night without us seeing him."

Dropping his pencil again, Hawkman took the letter.

"That doesn't make much sense. Why wouldn't he have broken in and taken care of you right then?"

"I don't know," she said, her voice tense. "Maybe because that cop kept circling the block."

"Did you show this note to anyone else?"

"No."

Hawkman eyed her suspiciously as he slipped the paper out of the envelope. He didn't like the way she ducked her head and wouldn't make eye contact. Something smelled fishy. He unfolded the sheet and glimpsed at the newspaper cut-outs glued across a piece of notebook paper. It read: 'You won't escape'. He glanced at her with skepticism. "So you think this is about your old boyfriend?"

"Of course." She screwed her mouth into a pout. "What else?"

"I don't know. That's why I'm asking you. Maybe something has happened in your world that might need to be kept quiet?"

She stiffened and sniffed indignantly. "What the hell do you think I am, a criminal?

Hawkman cleared his throat. "Sorry, didn't mean to sound offensive" He tossed the letter onto the desk. "There's that possibility you've stumbled across something no one wants revealed." In the back of his mind lingered the thought that an affair with a married man could bring on the wrath of a wife. "Any family problems?"

Her shoulders slumped. "My parents were killed years ago in an automobile accident. And you know about my aunt dying. I don't have any family left."

He furrowed his brow. "I'm sorry to hear that. You're awfully young to be without any relatives. How old are you?"

"Twenty-three going on forty." She flipped her hair behind her shoulder.

Hawkman shifted in his chair and balanced the yellow pad on his knee. "Okay, let's get back to the information I need for your file. I've only got your current address. Where did you live before moving to Medford? And I need your Social Security and driver's license numbers."

She straightened in her chair and looked puzzled. "Why

the hell do you need all that information? I'm going to pay you cash. You won't even have to claim it on your taxes."

"I don't operate that way, Ms. Schyler. I only want this information for my records. I don't plan on selling your name or Social Security number."

"What difference does it make where I lived before here? I can't see that has any bearing on me hiring you. If anything. I should be asking you those questions."

"Ask away, I'll answer anything within reason."

She waved a hand in the air. "Yeah, see there. Even you state 'within reason'. Just what does that mean?" She abruptly stood and hoisted her purse strap to her shoulder. "I don't need this."

Hawkman stared at the young woman for several moments, wondering what she was hiding. He picked up the note she'd presented and handed it to her. "This really isn't worth much as evidence. You've handled it and probably obliterated any finger prints. The cut-out letters from a newspaper could have been made by anyone." He looked her straight in the eyes. "Or you could have done this yourself."

Her eyes flared with fire as she snatched the paper from his hand. Cramming it back into her purse, she glared at him. "Like hell I did. Why would I write myself a threatening note? That doesn't even make sense." She turned in a huff and voiced over her shoulder, "I guess when they find me dead in some alley, you'll wish you'd helped me." Jamey Schyler slammed out of the office, leaving the aroma of cheap perfume lingering in the air.

Hawkman rubbed the stubble on his chin. "That's one feisty woman," he mumbled.

CHAPTER SIX

Hawkman tossed and turned in bed that night. Every time he closed his eyes Jamey Schyler's face popped into his mind. He studied the ceiling, thinking about the dumb note she'd probably concocted herself. Why go to all that trouble? Didn't she think I'd believe her without some form of tangible evidence? She actually seemed frightened over the guy following her and sincere about wanting to hire me. Then why wouldn't she give any information about her past. What is she hiding?

Unable to sleep, he finally sat up on the edge of the bed and slipped on his eye-patch. As he lifted his shoulder holster from the bedside table, the buckle rapped sharply against the wood. He cringed at the noise and glanced over at Jennifer. She opened her eyes and raised up on her elbow.

"Why are you up so early?"

"Sorry, didn't mean to wake you. Just couldn't sleep."

"Anything wrong?"

"No, try to get some rest. I'll talk to you later."

She yawned, rolled over and tucked the covers under her chin.

Hawkman carried his clothes into the living room, dressed, then turned on the coffee pot. He stared out the kitchen window and watched the beginning of a beautiful day as the sun peeked over the nearby hills. When the brew finished, he poured a cup and pondered his next move. The girl had offered him five hundred dollars to protect her. There must be something there he didn't see. Maybe he should drop by and talk to her. At least it would put his mind at ease.

Jennifer padded into the kitchen as he finished a bowl of cereal. "Is that all you're having this morning?" she asked.

"Yeah, I'm not hungry. This Jamey Schyler thing is bugging the hell out of me. Think I'll pay her a visit this morning. I feel there's more to the story than she's letting on."

Jennifer poured herself a mug of coffee and sat down at the kitchen bar opposite Hawkman. "Don't you think it's a little early. If the girl works at night, she's probably still asleep."

He sighed. "Yeah, you're right."

"Why don't you take Pretty Girl out for a morning hunt or run up and see Richard. You haven't been up there in quite awhile."

"Hey, that's a great idea. I could do both. It will certainly please Richard if the falcon still sits on his arm. Want to come?"

"I'd love to, but I'm so far behind. I better stay home and work on my articles. Give him my regards. Let me grab a blackberry pie from the freezer for him and Uncle Joe."

"Oh, man, they'll enjoy that."

While Jennifer went to the freezer in the garage, Hawkman slipped on the leather glove and retrieved Pretty Girl from the aviary out back. The bird seemed excited and flapped her long wings several times, which made it difficult for Hawkman to get her into the 4X4 and perched on her portable rack.

Jennifer stood behind him, patiently waiting with the pie wrapped in aluminum foil. "I think Pretty Girl's ready for a good hunt," she laughed.

He nodded, adjusting his hat that the falcon had knocked askew in her excitement. Giving Jennifer a peck on the cheek, he took the pie and climbed into the truck. "See ya in a few hours."

Hawkman beeped the horn when he glanced in the rear view mirror and saw her waving as he drove down the road.

When he approached the turn off to Richard's house, he couldn't believe his eyes. They had really cleaned up the place. The house sparkled with a new coat of paint; even the barn had been repaired and painted. By the time he pulled into the driveway, Richard had spotted him and came running out of the house, waving both arms, with a smile that shone like the sun.

Hawkman couldn't help but grin. The sight of the boy always gave him a warm feeling. "Hey Richard," he said, shaking his hand. "Looks like you and your uncle have really spruced up this place."

He nodded, and turned his gaze toward the falcon. "Are you taking her up to the knoll?"

"Yeah, want to come?"

"Yes!"

"Wait," Hawkman said, abruptly. "Shouldn't you be in school?"

"Winter break. Isn't Sam home?"

"No, he had to work. Hopefully he'll get to come home during the Spring vacation." He handed him Jennifer's pie and Richard dashed to the house to put it away. He returned within minutes, ready to go, with Uncle Joe at his heels.

"Tell Jennifer, 'thank you. We'll enjoy that treat," Joe called, as Richard jumped into the truck. Hawkman waved as he drove off toward the hill.

Richard's monotone voice, typical of a deaf person, no longer bothered Pretty Girl and she lifted from his arm without a problem. When the bird returned, Hawkman noticed the strength in the boy's shoulders as he barely flinched when she landed. He'd grown into a mature and handsome man in less than a year. His uncle had insisted that he finish his education at the public school and Richard would be graduating this year with top grades. Hawkman felt proud for the boy and knew he'd make it into college without a hitch.

He visited with Uncle Joe and Richard for an hour. They showed him the telephone they'd purchased for the deaf, along with the new double pane windows that had been installed throughout the house. They spoke excitedly about the new furniture coming for the living room and Uncle Joe's bedroom. Hawkman left the small farm, thankful that Jennifer had suggested the visit.

When he returned home around eleven, she greeted him with a kiss and pointed toward the kitchen bar where she had a sandwich waiting. "Thought you might be hungry after that meager breakfast. So, how'd the visit go?"

"Great, glad you suggested it. Richard's an awesome kid."

She smiled. "He has a good heart. I think of him every morning when I get up and put my bare feet on that rug."

❧

On the way to Medford, Hawkman turned on the police scanner. His stomach knotted when he heard the report of a young woman's body found in a field on the outskirts of town. She'd been shot in the head and abdomen. Jamey's last comment as she'd left the office yesterday echoed in his mind. His foot bore down on the accelerator.

At one o'clock, Hawkman rolled to a stop in front of the small cottage Jamey had inherited. Looking at the architecture and the old oak trees that surrounded the house, he figured it had been there for over fifty years. He strolled up the narrow cracked walkway that wound its way toward the front door. The screen door hung at an awkward angle, held in place by only one hinge near the top. He hadn't noticed that before; he'd check it out later.

As he stepped off the uneven four by four cement block that served as a front porch, he felt it shift under his weight. He headed for the rear of the house and glanced around the barren yard. The only signs of color were the green weeds protruding from the sidewalk and dandelions sticking out from each cracked concrete corner piling, their yellow heads bobbing in the breeze. Several empty beer cans littered the yard and the cottage definitely needed a coat of paint.

An empty car port made of poles and wind-whipped canvas leaned heavily against the outside wall. He knocked several times on the back door but received no answer, so he headed toward his truck, hesitating a few minutes before climbing inside. He knew Curly's didn't open until four, but decided he'd check it out anyway.

Driving through the alley behind the tavern, Hawkman noticed the back entrance was still padlocked. He exhaled loudly and figured he might as well head for the coroner's office. At least he'd find out the identity of the female corpse he'd heard about on the scanner. He drove out of the alley and circled the block in front of the bar just as Curly Spencer bustled out the door carrying a broom and dust pan. Hawkman pulled into a parking space.

He watched the stocky man with tufts of unruly white hair sticking out the back of his baseball cap, move tables and chairs off the slate patio. The man's shoulders were so wide that he must have his shirts specially made. If he hadn't been so short, he'd have made a great football player, Hawkman thought, chuckling to himself. Curly's Bar & Grill had been a part of Medford long before his arrival and had become locally famous for both its homemade recipe for hot wings and its friendly proprietor.

When Hawkman approached the robust guy he'd known for several years, Curly stopped sweeping and held out his hand, his eyes dancing with mischief.

"Hawkman, good to see ya. How's the private investigating business goin'?" He pointed a crooked finger at him. "You makin' lots of money?" He let out a belly laugh and playfully punched Hawkman's shoulder.

Hawkman grinned. "I like my job."

Curly chuckled. "So, you're tellin' me you ain't gettin' rich." He continued sweeping crumbs into the dust pan, gathering the debris from around the area, then threw it all into the nearby trash can. He brushed off his hands and glanced at Hawkman. "Heard you got yourself a new falcon."

"Yep, she's a beauty. Had her almost two years now. Took her out this morning. She loves to hunt."

"Bring her in some time. I'd like to see that bird."

"Will do."

Then he glanced at Hawkman with a dubious expression. "What brings you here before opening time?"

"Wanted to talk to you about Ms. Jamey Schyler."

He rolled his eyes. "Mark's new little honey. Hope she ain't in any trouble. Mark can't afford it." He gestured for Hawkman to follow him inside. "Wanta beer?"

"No, thanks. Too early for me. Any coffee made?"

"Yeah, sure." He hung the broom and dust pan in a closet, washed his hands, then poured them each a cup. Standing on the opposite side of the counter, he eyed Hawkman suspiciously. "Okay, what's the problem with Jamey?"

"Nothing, I hope. She came to my office yesterday wanting to hire me, but left in a huff. But, that's not what I wanted to talk to you about. She said some guy followed her night before last, so she came back here and got you."

"Yeah, I scouted around the area, didn't see a soul. Followed her home and made sure she got inside her house before I left. Never saw another car on the road comin' or goin'."

"She told me she'd run away from an abusive relationship and thought the guy had hired someone to find her. Has she ever mentioned this to you?"

Curly waved it off. "She told Mark and me that same story last night. But, I ain't seen anyone suspicious around here. We get a new face that hits the place now and then, but no one who acts strange or aggressive toward my girls. I'd kick them out if they did."

"Did she show you the anonymous threatening note?"

He frowned. "No. She never mentioned that."

"Have you seen her today?"

He shook his head. "Haven't seen her since last night. She took Mark home a little after midnight, cause his car's in the shop. I don't expect to see her again until work time."

"What kind of a vehicle does she drive?"

"An old blue Toyota Celica. Can't tell ya the year."

"Would you mind calling Mark and ask if he's talked to Jamey today?"

Curly raised a brow. "You've tried to reach her?"

Hawkman stuck a toothpick in his mouth. "Yeah, went by her place and she's not there."

"Give me a second." Curly hurried toward the end of the bar and disappeared into his private office, closing the door behind him. After a few minutes he emerged, his expression solemn. "Mark's been waiting a couple of hours for her to pick him up so he can go get his car. But he's worried because he can't reach her at home or on the cell phone." Curly shrugged. "Hey, you know women. She probably went to get her nails done and forgot all about Mark."

Hawkman thought about those long dagger fingernails Jamey sported. "Yeah, that's a good possibility. I'll check her place again." He stood. "Thanks for the coffee."

The stocky man scooted around the bar and followed him to the door. "Do you think something's happened to her?"

"Hope not," Hawkman said, his gut tightening at Curly's comment. He headed for his truck and drove away, the scanner rasping against his nerves as he listened for new information. He'd swing by the cottage one more time and if there were no signs of the girl, he'd go to the coroner's, a place he never took pleasure in visiting.

He approached the front of the cottage, but circled to the back. He exhaled in relief. The blue Toyota sat under the shade of the canvas with Jamey struggling to lift what looked like a full basket of laundry from the trunk. Before Hawkman could reach her, she tipped it over spilling some of the contents onto the dirt yard.

"Shit!" she exclaimed, throwing her purse inside the container of clothes. Swearing under her breath, she retrieved the garments from the ground, shaking each piece as she tossed it back into the basket. When Hawkman walked up and cleared his throat, she jumped, putting her hand to her throat. "My God, what the hell are you doing here. You scared me to death."

"Sorry. Guess you were pretty occupied with your laundry. Here let me help."

He picked up the basket and headed for the door as she threw a few more dust spotted items onto the top.

Pushing hair out of her face, she reached toward her side, then stopped abruptly. "Oh no! My purse is gone."

She dashed past him and headed for the car.

"Wait." Hawkman set down the basket and fished through the clothes until he uncovered the shoulder bag. He walked over to the car where she was frantically going through the interior, her butt in the air as she raked her hands under the seats.

"Uh, Ms. Schyler. Here it is."

She stood quickly almost knocking herself out against the door rim as she exited the car. "Damn," she cursed, rubbing the back of her head . "Where'd you find it?"

"In with your clean clothes. I think if you'd just slow down a minute, you might be safer."

She rolled her eyes. "Yeah, whatever!"

Hawkman flinched at the girl's hostility and wondered why he'd worried so much. She could handle any thug who crossed her.

Jamey yanked her house keys from her purse, then stumbled up a couple of steps to the back porch and unlocked the door. Hawkman, carrying the clothes, bumped into her when she suddenly stopped in the kitchen.

"Oh my God! I've been robbed!" she cried.

The cabinet drawers had been yanked out of their slots and their contents dumped. Chairs had been turned over and cans of food were rolling around on the floor.

"We didn't just have an earthquake, did we?" she asked, anxiously looking up at him.

Hawkman dropped the basket, pulled his gun and quickly stepped in front of her. "Get back. No earthquake did this. Someone might still be in the house."

She held onto the back of his shirt, chewing on the fingernails of her other hand as she followed him through the small house. Every room had been ransacked.

"Those damned little pot-smoking hoods. They're mad because I came on the scene. You saw all those roach clips and burned down candles that I cleaned out of here before moving in. It really puts a burr in their butts for me to be here," she raved. "If they think this will make me leave, they've got another think coming."

Hawkman had just stepped into her bedroom when Jamey let out a blood curdling scream.

CHAPTER SEVEN

Hawkman whirled around. Jamey had a fist to her mouth and pointed her other trembling hand toward the closet. His gun poised, he followed the direction of her shocked gaze. A black and white cat hung suspended from the clothes pole with a belt looped around its neck.

"Dear God," he gasped, holstering his gun. He quickly leaned into the wardrobe and removed the limp animal. Noting the warmth of its body, he gently placed the ball of fur on the floor and turned to Jamey. "I think the cat's still alive. Her paw was caught in the belt around her neck and probably saved her. Rub her belly and try to force some air into the lungs."

Jamey knelt beside the kitten and blew gently into its mouth while massaging its stomach and chest. "Why the hell did some son-of-a-bitch hurt my Mitzi?" she sobbed. "She never did anything to anybody."

Hawkman left her and continued checking the house. In the living room, he noticed the chair that had sat in front of the door appeared to have been scooted forward. On further investigation, he discovered the flimsy lock on the entry had been jimmied. Not wanting to smudge any possible prints, he went through the kitchen and out the back door. He circled to the front where he checked the surrounding yard but found no visible footprints on the hard pan ground. Now he knew why the screen hung by one hinge.

He went back inside and found Jamey sitting on the edge of the bed holding a wiggling cat. She looked up and smiled. "I think she's going to be all right."

"Glad to hear it." Rubbing his chin, he stared at Jamey.

"Ms. Schyler, it's not safe for you to stay in this house. Do you have a friend you could hang out with for a few days?"

She shrugged. "Maybe. I'll have to check around. But I need to clean this place first."

He raised his hand and shook his head. "No, I don't want you to touch a thing right now."

She frowned. "Why? It's probably just a bunch of those idiot no-good kids getting back at me for moving in here. I've yelled at them many times and threatened to call the cops, but I never did."

Hawkman removed the cell phone from his belt. "Regardless, I'm notifying the authorities of the break in." He hit the dial button for the police station and put the phone to his ear. "This is Tom Casey. I want to report a B & E, possible theft and animal abuse." After giving the address he hung up and turned back to Jamey. "I want this place dusted for prints, and I want you out of here as soon as possible."

She narrowed her eyes. "You don't have any right to tell me what to do."

He glared at her. "No, you're right. I came over here to talk to you about your case." He waved a hand over the mess. "But after seeing this, I'd like to take it on. That is, if you're still interested in hiring me."

Leaving the feline playing with a towel, Jamey stomped into the living room, folded her arms across her chest and stared out the front window. Soon, she dropped her hands to her side and let out a sigh. "Here come the cops."

Hawkman had developed a camaraderie with the police department and knew most of the officers. He quickly went outside and directed the men through the back door, while explaining to Officer Clancy, one of the veterans, what had happened. Hawkman suggested they dust for prints and Clancy immediately got on the radio to put through the order.

When the lab van arrived, Jamey grabbed the cat and Hawkman escorted her to the yard, where they leaned against the fender of his 4X4 for several minutes before either spoke. Jamey frowned while caressing Mitzi and watching the activity going on around the house.

Hawkman pushed away from the truck and hooked his thumbs in his jeans front pockets. "Ms. Schyler, I know you told me that you believed a bunch of hoodlums did this, but do you have any other enemies besides Carl Hopkins?"

She shot him a frustrated look. "Good Lord! I haven't been here long enough to make enemies, except for those no good kids. So get off my back. I told you yesterday Carl's the one who concerns me, but you don't believe my story."

"I never said that. I talked with Curly earlier today and he said there had been no strangers hanging around the work place."

She shot him a look. "You talked to Curly?"

He nodded. "Yeah."

She turned her back to him in disgust. "He thinks I'm an air head. He'd just as soon Mark didn't associate with me."

"Speaking of Mark, did you get in touch with him?"

She furrowed her brow. "What for?"

"Weren't you supposed to take him to pick up his car at the garage?"

A look of agony swept across her face. "Oh my God! I went to do my laundry and completely forgot about that." Handing the cat to Hawkman, she hurried toward the house. "I better call him."

"Hold on," Hawkman shouted. "Don't go inside. Use your cell phone."

"I don't know where it is," she yelled over her shoulder.

Fumbling to reach his own on his belt while trying to hold a wiggling cat, he called, "Use mine." He could already tell this woman would drive him nuts.

She raced back, grabbed the phone, then walked a short distance away. When she ended her conversation, she slipped it into her pocket. Hawkman snapped his fingers and held out his hand.

"Oh, sorry," she said, grinning slyly, and took Mitzi while handing him the phone. "Oh, by the way, Mark said I could stay at his place until this blows over."

The technicians finally finished their job and filed out of

the house. One of the men with a clipboard headed toward Hawkman and Jamey. After a few questions, he left.

Then Clancy approached them and filled out the police report. "Ms. Schyler, I'm sure you haven't had time to check and see what's missing. As soon as you know, give us a call." Then he addressed Hawkman. "I'll be getting in touch with you as soon as I have anything."

"Sounds good," Hawkman waved, as he followed Jamey back into the house. He still wondered if the girl wanted him to take the case. Something fishy was definitely taking place. She should count herself lucky for not being here when this happened. "Okay, Ms. Schyler," he said in a steely voice. "I want you to leave right now."

She dropped the cat to the floor and put her hands on her hips as she surveyed the kitchen. "I don't even know if anything has been stolen yet and I can't leave this clutter."

"You know, that could have been you hanging in that closet instead of the cat, and you might not have been as lucky. Do you want to take that chance?"

Her eyes filled with fear as she stared at him. "Are you serious? You really think my life is in danger?"

"Yes."

Her hand trembled as she picked up a can of corn off the floor and set it on the counter. "Then to hell with this mess. I have very few valuables and it'll only take me a few minutes to check if they're still here."

"If you want me to take this case, I will. But you're going to have to heed my warnings and follow instructions."

She rubbed her hands down her jeans. "I appreciate your offer, Mr. Casey, but I don't think I need a private investigator and I truly can't afford one. I jumped too fast the other day because it frightened me that someone would follow me that late at night. But it hasn't happened again and I've settled down."

"Are you secure with the feeling that the ransacking of your house and the guy who followed you aren't connected?"

"Oh, I'm almost positive that bunch of kids did this.

Hurting Mitzi is right down their alley. It has nothing to do with whoever followed me the other night."

"I still think you better pack up a few things and vacate the house for three or four days. Let this blow over before moving back in."

She waved a hand toward the window. "Once these kids hear about all the police around this place, they won't be back. But I'll do as you wish. However, not for long," she said, wagging a finger in the air.

"I'll wait outside in the truck, then follow you to Mark's."

Nodding, she headed toward the bedroom as Hawkman went out the door.

༺

Jasmine Louise Schyler had a hunch that Mr. Casey knew she'd lied and when she refused to give him any information, he probably suspected she was hiding something. Of course, being a nosy private detective, he might discover things on his own. But she'd deal with that when it happened.

Right now, she'd stick with her story until she felt out of danger from Carl. She'd journeyed to Oregon hoping to leave that man behind forever. Gnawing her lower lip, she threw what few belongings she cared about into a bag. Thankful the diamonds were hidden in the car, she ran her hand under her pillow and breathed a sigh of relief when she found the small gun still there. Her eyes narrowed as she flipped on the safety and dropped it into her purse. She glanced around the room and decided the kids must have stolen the cell phone. Then she remembered putting it beside her last night. She reached over and tossed back the bed covers. Sure enough it had slipped down near the foot. She clipped it to her jeans' waist band, grabbed her purse and clothes, picked up the cat with her free hand, then headed out the back toward the blue Toyota. She waved at Hawkman and yelled. "I found everything." Then she jumped into the car.

Jamey watched the big 4X4 in her rear view mirror pull behind her as she turned onto the road. She had to admit that

Mr. Casey made her feel safe, but she couldn't afford to have a private investigator poking around in her life.

She let out a sigh as her thoughts drifted to Mark. A night or two with him might be okay, but any longer would grate on her nerves. However, she'd accept this temporary situation and move back into her house as soon as possible.

Then her thoughts turned to Carl Hopkins. Cold fear slipped up her spine and a sharp tic erupted on her right cheek. If he showed up before she had a chance to get away, she'd kill him and claim self-defense.

ॐ

Down near the creek, leaning against a large oak tree, Nick Albergetti, a pair of small binoculars to his eyes, watched the action taking place at the small house and wondered about the big guy with the eye-patch. How did he fit into the picture? He obviously wasn't a cop, but something about his manner made Nick apprehensive. Not many men could do that.

He'd gone through every corner of that house and found nothing. The cat had followed him around meowing until he had to string it up. He couldn't stand furry creatures anyway. Somehow, the animal must have gotten loose, as he noticed Jamey carrying it as she came out of the house. Looks like he'd have to talk to that pretty little gal and do some persuading to find those diamonds. He slipped the binoculars into his pocket, snickering as he walked toward his car.

CHAPTER EIGHT

Mark slid his arm around the waist of the slim naked body lying next to him. "Oh, baby you're good," he said, kissing the butterfly tattoo on her bare shoulder.

She groaned. "You are too, Mark, but I need some rest."

"Hey, is that all you have to say after all that passion?"

Yanking up the blanket to cover herself, she scooted out of his reach and rolled over, putting her back toward him. "Please, honey, let me get some sleep. I have a lot on my mind."

"Okay, sweetheart. I understand." He nuzzled her ear and whispered a few suggestive words.

"Mark, will you just hush up and get out of here. You know I have to work tonight."

He climbed out of bed and raised his hands in mock defense. "Okay, okay, I'm going." He stared at the long blond hair flowing over the pillow, then grabbed his clothes from the chair and eased out of the room, closing the door softly behind him. The apartment consisted of one bedroom, a compact kitchen and small living room. He stood a moment with his hand on the knob wondering if such close quarters would ruin this relationship.

In just a short time, he'd become fascinated with this feisty female who had a mind of her own and loved her independence. He feared she didn't share his same feelings.

Jamey had been closed mouthed about her past, but mentioned she'd grown up in Oklahoma. His dad, Curly, had mumbled that he thought his son could do better than a cocktail waitress. Yet he admired Jamey's loyalty. He'd commented how her good looks had pulled in new customers and often compared her to Mark's mother who had worked hard all her life holding a variety of jobs. She'd passed away several years ago and his dad missed her terribly.

Mark took a deep breath and checked the time. He needed about thirty minutes to drive into Ashland for his classes at the Southern Oregon College. It wouldn't be long now before he had his degree. As he sat in the quiet of the kitchen having a bowl of cold cereal and a cup of coffee, Mitzi tumbled around his feet playing with his shoe strings.

Carl Hopkins called the apartment numerous times from his hospital room, but only got the squeal of the filled answering machine which had stopped taking messages. He slammed down the receiver, sat up and swung his legs over the edge of the bed. The doctor had released him this morning and it ticked him off that he couldn't reach Jamey, which meant he'd have to take a cab home. Where had she gone? Surely she'd read the papers or heard the news and knew that no charges had been pressed. So, why the hell hadn't she visited him at the hospital? After all he'd done for her; paid her rent and bills, then let her keep her own paycheck so she could buy those tacky silk dresses she loved. He shook his head and muttered, "The woman's beautiful, but has no class."

He shifted his weight, trying to get comfortable. The cloth sling had a strap around his middle to hold his left arm immobile. Right now his shoulder ached like hell.

Carl exhaled loudly as he reluctantly called a cab and rang for the nurse. He gathered what few possessions he had from the cabinet and threw them into a plastic bag furnished by a volunteer. The nurse arrived with a wheelchair, pushed him to the street curb where she helped him into the cab, wished him good luck, then disappeared behind the automatic doors of the hospital. Carl called out the address from the back seat. When they arrived, he handed the cabby the fare and a dollar tip. The driver grunted.

"Hey buddy, be happy you got that. You just took my last dollar. Don't spend it all in one place."

Carl climbed out of the taxi and headed for the apartment. When he unlocked the door and tried to open it, he found it wouldn't budge. "What the...," he mumbled, pushing harder. He peered through the crack and discovered mail had piled up behind the slot and wedged under the bottom edge. He gave a hard shove with his good shoulder and forced a big enough opening to wiggle his leg through, but grimaced at the effort. "Careful," he said aloud. "Gotta watch out not to strain anything."

He kicked the letters away and finally got inside. Slamming the door, he dropped the plastic bag onto the coffee table, and picked up several of the envelopes scattered across the floor. Some were marked with final red notices such as rent past due and threats to shut off power and water.

"What the hell," he yelled. "Jamey always kept the bills paid."

He threw them onto the table and hurried toward the bedroom. Stunned, he stood for a moment, as his gaze swept the room. The opened closet revealed several bare hangers, and her empty dresser drawers hung wide open. He crossed over to the bathroom. She'd cleaned out the medicine cabinet and the toilet tank top showed only the rings of make-up containers.

Carl slapped his right hand against the bathroom wall. "You bitch!!" He sat on the edge of the bed to catch his breath. When the realization hit him that she'd obviously left with the stash of diamonds, he felt a wave of exhaustion pass over him. It would take a few days to get back his strength after the hospital stay, but he vowed right then and there that he'd find her. When he did, there'd be hell to pay. He eased down on his right side and slowly turned onto his back.

After a short nap, he awoke refreshed, went to the kitchen and heated up a can of soup. He ate, then sorted through the stack of mail. When he spotted the bill for the gasoline card, he ripped it open and glanced through the charges.

"Ah ha," he said aloud. His finger followed Jamey's trek west. The last entry on this bill indicated she'd filled the car's tank in Arizona. He went to retrieve his laptop computer from the closet only to discover it gone.

"Dammit!" he cursed. "She took that too."

Going into the living room, he booted up the PC and logged in on that account and checked the latest entries. They ended in Los Angeles. "Shit," he muttered. "That's a big place." He flipped through the remaining bills and found Jamey's bank statement. Typing in the number and password, he prayed she hadn't changed it. Exhaling a breath of relief, he watched the display of transactions form on the screen, but then he noted the zero balance. Why had she pulled out a thousand dollars in two days? Could it have dawned on her that she'd left an electronic trail he could follow? If so, this little broad has more brains than he thought.

Digging out a map of California, he spread it out on the table and put his finger on Los Angeles where her trail ended. Would she stay there? He doubted she'd like that area. But she'd need a job sooner or later. He leaned back in the chair and tapped his chin with his finger. Unless she decided to pawn one or more of the diamonds. They were marked and could be traced. That could put her in real danger of getting arrested.

The thought made him nervous and he immediately turned back to the computer, pulled up the Los Angeles Police Department and went into recent arrests. He scoured the list and saw nothing about stolen diamonds or Jamey's name. Relieved, he exited the site and shut down. Surely, since she'd worked in a jewelry store, she'd be aware of diamond markings. That alone should make her think twice before attempting to sell any. But he knew Jamey's impulsiveness and she might try something, regardless of the consequences. Also he knew if she got caught with the stolen gems, she'd implicate him.

Slapping his hand on the table, he muttered. "I've got to get to her before she makes a dumb mistake." Then he snapped his fingers. Tina Randolph, her best girlfriend lived in Los Angeles. He yanked open the drawer under the phone where Jamey kept the address book, but it was gone. He searched through what things were left in the bedroom, but found nothing.

Slumping down on the couch in the living room, rubbing his arm and shoulder that ached from the exertion, it dawned on him, she might have put Tina's number into the memory bank of her personal phone. He reluctantly got up, made his way back to the bedroom and sat down on her side of the bed. Searching the list of names she'd written on the phone card, he found Tina's and copied the number. He slipped it into his wallet, then laid back on the pillows, picked up the receiver and hit the number two button.

The next day, Carl left the doctor's office in a huff. The physician warned him not to drive across country and said he wouldn't take responsibility if he did. The doctor gave permission for him to fly, but Carl's funds were drying up. Buying an airline ticket and renting a car would leave him with almost nothing. To hell with the doctor's opinion. He'd take his chances.

He wished his contacts for fencing gems extended as far west as California. Then he'd just stay out there. But without such connections, he'd have to return to Oklahoma. Damn, Jamey had ended up causing him more problems than she was worth. Now he wished he'd just done the heist on his own. However, if she hadn't fled with the jewels, they'd have found them on him and he'd be doing time. So, he had to be grateful for that. But now he must find her.

He'd left a message on Tina's answering machine, but she hadn't returned his call. If Jamey had visited her, she'd more than likely been warned about talking to him. He'd try again later.

Inside the truck, Carl discovered the tote bag Jamey had left from the robbery. He removed the brass knuckles and scrubbed them with soap and water, then returned them to the glove box in case of an emergency. He searched under the seat and mat for the keys, but couldn't find them. Fortunately, he had another set, so didn't think much more about it. He packed a duffel bag, placed it in the back seat of the Toyota King cab, locked up the apartment, then headed down the highway for Los Angeles.

Jamey waited until Mark left before she got up and dressed. In the bathroom, she leaned over to slip on her shoes and hit her butt on the sink, almost impelling her head-on into the wall. She exhaled loudly. Her cottage wasn't big, but this apartment gave her claustrophobia. Regardless of what Mr. Tom Casey said, she intended to move back home today.

She wasn't worried about those kids coming back. Once they knew about all the police activity around her place yesterday, they'd keep their distance. She threw her clothes together and scribbled a note to Mark. She could hardly wait to get back home and put the place in order.

The minute she entered the cottage, she dropped her purse on the kitchen table, placed Mitzi on the floor, and put her bag of clothes in the bedroom. She picked up the canned goods scattered across the floor, ran some hot soapy water into the sink and soon had the kitchen clean again. Pushing ringlets of sweaty hair behind her ears, she went to the hall closet and dragged out the old upright vacuum.

She plugged it in and turned on the noisy contraption. Concentrating on pushing it across the carpet, she didn't hear the back door open. Suddenly, a hand gripped her arm. She shrieked and whirled around, swinging the vacuum into the groin of the intruder, knocking him on his butt.

Staring down at the man, she flipped off the vacuum and put her hand to her mouth. "What the hell are you doing here?"

CHAPTER NINE

That same morning, Jennifer studied Hawkman's pensive expression from across the breakfast table until she couldn't stand it any longer. "You're awfully quiet."

Hawkman glanced up, holding a bite of sausage on his fork. "I'm bored. No cases right now."

"What about the Jamey Schyler thing?"

"Oh, she's a little foul mouthed spitfire."

Jennifer chuckled. "Sounds like a gal who knows how to push your buttons."

He grinned. "I have to agree. I cringe every time she opens her mouth. And she'd just as soon tell the law to go to hell as abide by it."

"Well, women are getting more assertive all the time."

He nodded. "Boy, you got that right. Her cock and bull story bothered me so much that I stopped by her place to ask a few questions and came upon more than I expected." He then told Jennifer about the ransacked house and half strangled cat. "After witnessing that chaos, I figured she did need help."

"Sounds like she might be right about rowdy kids taking revenge on her for moving into their playhouse."

"True. And she definitely has the guts to give them a piece of her mind. Clancy mentioned there had been a rash of break-ins and cases of animal brutality in that area." He finished the bite of meat, then leaned back in his chair and stared at Jennifer. "You ever thought about getting a belly button ring?"

Her mouth dropped open. "Good heavens! I've never thought of such a thing. Whatever brought that on?"

"Jamey has one." He raised a brow and grinned. "Not bad, in fact, it's kinda sexy."

Jennifer stood and put her hands on her hips. "Tom Casey, that's enough out of you. How do you know that Jamey has a belly button ring?"

"She had on jeans and a short top when she came into my office. The little gold ring glowed in all its glory."

Jennifer's eyes narrowed. "You ought to be ashamed of yourself."

Hawkman threw back his head and laughed. "I sure know how to push your buttons."

She threw her napkin at him. "You're terrible."

He wiped the tears of laughter from his eyes. "Oh my, I wish you could see your face. You look like a jealous tigress ready to bounce."

She grinned. "Well, you can rest assured that this lady won't be getting a belly button ring, regardless of how sexy you might think it is. And if you're taking this case, you can bet I'll be tailing you."

Hawkman laughed again. "Don't worry, hon. She didn't hire me. I thought since I don't have anything going right now, that we might take a trip down south and visit some sights. Even stop by and see old Claude. He's been after us to come down and fish his bass pond for a long time."

"I'd love that, but I can't leave right now. I'm working on some deadlines with my wildlife articles and I'm way behind. It will be a couple of weeks or more before I get them done. Maybe we can do it then."

"Okay, sounds good. But I'm holding you to your word," he said in a mock gruff voice.

Hawkman headed for Medford so that Jennifer could work at the computer without interruption. When he reached his office, he sat down at his desk and forced himself to insert the final entries into his ledger. After several hours, he slammed the book shut and breathed a sigh of relief. "Finally got that done," he mumbled. "Now if the IRS wants to audit me, I'm ready."

He checked his watch and decided to run by Jamey's place

to make sure no one was messing around before picking up the grocery list Jennifer had handed him. Locking up the office, he headed out.

When he arrived at the cottage, he spotted Jamey's car parked out back, alongside another car. It appeared she had company. She'd acted pretty anxious to get the place cleaned up and didn't seem to fear that the perpetrator might return. She must have talked a friend into helping.

He debated whether to stop, but decided to check and see if everything was okay. Approaching the back door, he could hear Jamey's frightened voice.

"I don't know what you're talking about."

When she screamed and Hawkman heard something slam against the wall, he pulled his gun and yanked open the door. A man stood in the doorway leading into the living room with one arm looped around Jamey's neck, threatening her with the gun he held in his other hand. When Hawkman advanced, the man whirled her around in front of him and pointed the weapon at her head.

"Drop it or I'll kill her."

Hawkman stepped back, put his gun on the kitchen table and raised his hands. The man dragged a struggling Jamey toward the kitchen entry. As they passed Hawkman, she sobbed. "Mr. Casey, do something. He's going to kill me."

Jamey still in his grasp, the man stepped backward toward the door, but Mitzi's howl caused him to jerk his head around. In that split moment, Hawkman grabbed his gun from the table and leaped forward. In a flash, he yanked Jamey out of the man's grasp, and brought the butt of his gun down hard. He missed his target when the man twisted out of the way and the blow glanced off his shoulder.

He swung around and plastered a wallop to Hawkman's jaw that knocked off his hat and sent him reeling. Jamey hovered in the corner on the floor, hugging her knees to her chest, tears rolling down her cheeks. Suddenly, she screamed, "Casey, look out!"

Hawkman shook his head and spun on his heel to see the

barrel of the man's gun aimed at his head. He grabbed one of the kitchen stools, and heaved it toward the intruder just as a bullet whizzed by his ear. Dropping to the floor, Hawkman rolled under the table, leveling his gun at the stranger's heart; but before he could pull the trigger, another shot echoed through the air. The man hit the wall and slid to the floor.

Hawkman twisted around to see Jamey with a smoking Beretta pistol in her hand. Jumping to his feet, his gun still poised, he approached the fallen body. Kicking the man's gun out of reach, he bent over and felt for a pulse. He couldn't find one.

Rubbing his jaw, Hawkman holstered his gun, took the cell phone from his belt and dialed 911. He then turned to Jamey who sat curled up and whimpering against the wall, the gun dangling from her fingers. A small trickle of blood flowed from the corner of her mouth. He knelt on his haunches, gently removed the Beretta from her hand and placed it on the table, then put his fingers under her chin forcing her to look up. "You okay?"

She nodded, rubbing her fingers over her lips. "I think so, except my mouth hurts where he slapped me."

He helped her up. "Get some ice on it."

She went to the refrigerator, took out a tray from the freezer and dumped it on the counter. Wrapping the chunks in a towel, she slumped down in a chair beside the table and applied the cold pack to her mouth.

Hawkman pointed at the gun. "Where the hell did you get that?"

Jamey glared at him, but sat silently, holding the compress.

He then nodded toward the corpse. "Who is he and what did he want?"

She glanced up at him with fearful eyes and shook her head. "I don't know. He came to Curly's the other night and flirted with me. Told me to call him Nick. That's the only time I'd ever seen him until today."

Hawkman heard the sirens and glanced out the window. Two black and whites rolled up to the house and Detective Williams followed in his unmarked car.

He let the police in and gave a quick run down of what had occurred. After the initial investigation, Williams placed a call to the coroner, then gave instructions to his officers. He turned to Jamey and directed her to go into the living room, along with Hawkman. The detective followed and sat down on the couch beside Jamey. Hawkman took the over-stuffed chair near the door.

Williams pulled the evidence bag from his pocket that contained the Beretta pistol and held it toward Jamey "This belong to you?"

Her eyes narrowed as she glared at the detective. "Yes. I have a permit. I'm the registered owner and know how to use it."

"Where'd you get your permit?"

"Oklahoma," she said curtly.

"Don't get huffy. But I'll warn you. Oregon doesn't honor Oklahoma's permit to carry a concealed weapon, so don't get any ideas."

"The gun wasn't concealed. It was on my kitchen table. I'd just cleaned it," she lied.

"Ms. Schyler, this is very disturbing. You've had two threatening incidents occur in a very short time. You say this man appeared at Curly's and now he's here, dead on your kitchen floor. But yet you claim you don't know him. And you shot him with your gun. It all sounds a bit far fetched. Appears to me, he hunted you down for a reason. And I'd like to know why."

She glanced at Hawkman. "I'd never seen that man until he came into Curly's. I shot him in self-defense. Mr. Casey can swear to that. Otherwise, he'd have killed us both." She glared at the detective. "You make me sound like some sort of criminal."

"Sorry, don't mean to imply that. I'll check with Curly for verification."

Jamey continued. "While you're at it, ask him about the night I came back to the bar scared half out of wits because someone had followed me from work. Then talk to one of your officers who questioned a man sitting in a car with his lights off, right out there in front of my house." She pointed toward the road. "Maybe he can identify him as the same guy I just shot."

"I'll do that." He took a pad of paper from his pocket and scribbled some notes. "Did others see this man at the bar?"

"Oh, yes. All the waitresses were going nuts over the good looking guy who'd just walked in the door. Just wait until they find out what happened." She shivered outwardly. "It gives me the willies to think about what he might have had on his mind."

Williams stood. "Okay, Ms. Schyler. That's about all I need from you now. Don't leave town without notifying me."

"Where the hell would I go?" she said, looking up at him in disgust.

He shrugged and headed for the door. "Hawkman, you interested in finding out about the deceased? If so, you're welcome to join me at the morgue."

"Yeah. I'll be there in a few minutes."

But before he got out the door, Jamey said. "Hawkman?"

He swung around. "Yeah."

Jamey raised a finely arched eyebrow and looked at him with a puzzled expression. "Hawkman?"

He laughed. "Yeah, that's me. I just assumed you'd heard my nickname by now."

"No. How'd you ever get stuck with that?"

He quickly told her about the falcons as she listened intently.

"Can I call you Hawkman?" she asked, slyly. "I like it a lot better than Mr. Casey."

He grinned. "Sure."

She pushed her hair behind her ears and wiped her face with her hands. "I better get myself together before work."

"Why don't you stay home? I'm sure Curly would understand."

"I'm too nervous to stay here alone."

"Do you think Carl Hopkins is out there?"

"I don't know. But he's probably the one who sent that guy to find me."

"What kind of a vehicle does Hopkins' drive? I'll keep an eye out for him."

"A black Toyota Tacoma. I don't know the year, but fairly new." With that, she stepped into her bedroom and closed the door.

He rubbed his chin in thought, then flinched at his own touch, realizing he had a very sore jaw. He left her house and headed for the morgue. Then he intended to do some digging on his own. Jamey Louise Schyler had piqued his interest.

He drove to the morgue and had just turned off the ignition when the detective came out the door. "Hey, Williams," he called out the window. "Did you find out the identity of that dude?"

He held up a clear bag. "So far, all I've got is a billfold and driver's license under the name of Nick Albergetti. I'm going back to my office to verify it and see what else I can find out."

"I'll give you a call later." Hawkman started his truck and drove away, thinking about the research he had in mind. This whole Jamey Schyler affair had him intrigued.

Jamey watched Hawkman leave from her bedroom window, then sat down on the edge of the bed, her insides trembling. There was no way she would have admitted to Hawkman or the detective that Nick's questioning her about the diamonds and her refusal to answer was the reason he bounced her off the wall.

If Hawkman hadn't made his appearance, Nick could have killed her. She shuddered at the thought and felt chilled to the bone, even though beads of sweat were forming on her upper lip. Who was this Nick and how did he know about the diamonds? Who else knew about the gems? Would there be more trying to find her?

All these questions firing through her brain made her very nervous. She quickly made her way through every room and locked the doors and closed the drapes. How she wished the detective hadn't taken her gun.

CHAPTER TEN

When Hawkman unlocked the door and stepped into his office, a wave of muggy air hit him in the face. Warmer days were definitely on the way. He flipped on the fan of the air conditioner to freshen the room and opened the window to let the warmth escape. Glancing up at the tattered dove's nest under the eaves, he grinned to see the female busily maneuvering the twigs as her mate brought in new ones.

It only took a few minutes for the room to get comfortable, so he flipped off the fan, but left the window open. Of course, then he could smell the donut shop below. He tried to push the tempting aroma out of his mind as he sat down at the computer. But it didn't work. The temptation finally got the better of him. He jumped up, put on a fresh pot of coffee then sprinted down the steps to the bakery.

With two of the freshly made delicacies in hand, he returned to his office, poured a mug of coffee and settled behind the desk. Now, he was ready to find out about Jasmine Louise Schyler. He typed her name into a search engine, but to his amazement, nothing came up. "That's odd," he mumbled.

Next, he brought up the newspaper of the small Oklahoma town where Jamey's aunt had moved to and typed in Rachel Smith. Her obituary popped up and Hawkman thought it interesting that the only living relative listed was Jasmine Louise Gray. His curiosity rose even more. Why would Jamey change her last name?

He went to the city's home page and discovered that the current sheriff had worked in this same community for years. Often in these rural towns, the police knew most of the people personally. He hoped Jamey's family had stayed around that same area. Possibly, the sheriff could shed some light on her past. He decided to give him a call and dialed the listed number.

When Sheriff Monahan came on line, Hawkman gave his credentials before explaining the reason for the call. "I'm doing a background search on a young woman that lived in your locale several years ago. Her name is Jasmine Louise Schyler. She goes by the nickname Jamey. Do you by chance remember her?"

"Schyler, Schyler," the man repeated. "The only Schylers I remember were an older couple who are now deceased."

"Do they have any relatives nearby?"

"They might have a daughter." He hesitated a moment. "No, that's not right. I remember now, they were childless, but they took in a young girl whose parents were killed in an automobile accident."

"Do you remember the people's name who were killed?" Hawkman asked.

"If my memory serves me right, I believe it was Gray."

"Thank you, Sheriff, appreciate your help."

Hawkman hung up, his hand resting on the phone for a few moments before his attention went back to the computer. He typed Jasmine Louise Gray into the search block. This time, the data unfolded: when and where she was born, along with minor information. He noted she'd been cited a couple of times for speeding, but had paid off the tickets. Nothing showed any serious brushes with the law. Her current address was listed as Oklahoma City. He found no indication that she'd been married or legally changed her name. While printing out the information, he sat back and studied the screen. Jamey had told him the partial truth about her parent's death, but had been careful not to mention their name.

He exited that web page and went to National Newspapers, opened up Oklahoma, then clicked on the paper called, 'The Oklahoman'. Going to the archives, he put in Carl Hopkins' name and watched the monitor with interest. It only took a few seconds before the dates of the news items appeared.

Clicking on the link to the first article, he read it, printed it out, then continued searching through the other mentioned editions. One column in particular made him sit upright, sending a surge of adrenalin rushing through his veins.

While the article printed, he called the Regency Hotel in Oklahoma City and asked for the registration desk. After several minutes of questioning the clerk, he hung up, snatched up the printed material and headed out the door. Hawkman drove quickly to the police department. Racing up the steps of the building, he almost collided with Detective Williams coming out the door.

"Hey, hold on there, big guy, don't run me down," the detective said, laughing.

"Sorry about that. You're just the man I came to see."

"If you're wondering about Albergetti, all I can tell you is he's an ex-con. Served time for check forgery and is highly suspected as a small time scam artist. However, he's never been convicted on any of those crimes yet. The only phone number I found in the wallet belonged to his cell phone. No evidence of his being married. And the address listed on the license is bogus. So gonna have to do some deeper checking."

"That's all interesting. But it's not what I came to see you about."

Williams frowned and hooked a thumb toward the door. "Do we have to go back into the office?"

Hawkman shook his head. "No."

Williams wiped his brow in fake relief. "Good, It's been a long day and I'm ready for a beer."

"Let's take my truck. Where'd you like to go?"

"How about Curly's?"

"Uh, let's skip Curly's and go on downtown. You'll understand after I explain."

The detective glanced at him with a questioning eye. "Nothing coming from you surprises me."

They ended up at a pizza parlor, ordered and carried their beers to a booth at the far corner of the room.

Williams held up his drink, took a large gulp, then grinned. "Ah, that's good." He wiped his mouth with the back of his hand. "Now, you can tell me what's on your mind."

Hawkman pushed up the brim of his cowboy hat with his index finger. "This is about Jamey Schyler. First of all, I'll let you know I got fired before I even got my first check."

Williams laughed. "So you're doing this on your own time? Boy, you must get a damned good retirement from the Agency."

Grinning, Hawkman nodded. "Let's just say, I'm comfortable." He then gave the detective a run down of the story that Jamey had told him at his office. "I didn't swallow the tale at first, but now part of it's coming together. However, her problem with Carl Hopkins isn't an 'abusive relationship' like she tried to make me believe. Instead, I think she's involved in a robbery."

The detective raised a bushy brow. "Oh yeah, how much?"

"Not dollars. Diamonds."

Williams started to pick up his beer, but set it back down. "Diamonds! Here in Medford?" He poked the table with his finger.

The two men stopped talking until the waitress finished serving their pizza, then moved out of earshot.

"No, back in Oklahoma." Hawkman said, pulling a folded paper from his pocket. "I found this article in one of the newspapers back there. Carl Hopkins got involved in a messy situation at the Regency Hotel in Oklahoma City with a diamond courier. It states Hopkins barged into the man's room by mistake. The two scuffled and Hopkins somehow managed to break this Bob Evans' jaw before the guy shot him. Hopkins has been recovering in the hospital and Evans claims some of his gems are missing."

The detective scowled and turned the paper over. "I don't see a date here. When did this incident take place?"

"About six weeks ago." Hawkman pointed his finger at the printout. "I think Jasmine Louise Schyler, aka Jasmine Louise Gray, was involved in that heist."

Williams glanced at him over the top of his reading glasses. "Jasmine Louise Gray?"

"Yeah. That's her real name. I figure she changed to Schyler to foil Carl Hopkins' search."

The detective waved his hand over the paper. "The article doesn't mention anyone else. And they didn't find any diamonds on Hopkins or in his room." He shook his finger in the air. "You know this courier might be trying to pull a slick one."

"That thought occurred to me too, until I ran across this." He handed him the other clipping. "Read the second paragraph."

Williams read aloud. "The desk clerk stated a woman accompanied Mr. Hopkins when he checked into the hotel. He figured her for a hooker, which Hopkins confirmed later, but stated she left an hour before the incident and he never knew her name. The authorities haven't been able to locate the woman."

The detective eyed him intently. "I see where you're going with this. You think the girl was Jamey what's-her-name?"

Hawkman nodded. "Exactly. I talked to the clerk who worked the desk that night in question and his description of the woman matches Jamey. They found Hopkins bleeding and unconscious on the floor of the neighboring room. I think he managed to get back in there and gave her the diamonds. She then high tailed it out the back way and disappeared before anyone saw her."

Williams wiped his mouth with a napkin. "Very interesting. But why hasn't the diamond company made a stink? We usually get something through the station if they've lost a big haul."

"Maybe they're keeping a lid on it right now and doing an internal investigation. You know they're bound to be questioning that courier. The insurance company might want to give their special agents time to come up with something before they send out a notice. Precious gems are insured to the hilt and I doubt they relish the idea of having to deal out that kind of money on a swindle."

"I agree," Williams said, handing back the printout. "If something does pop up in regards to this, we'll work together. Of course, I can't pay you."

Hawkman grinned and nodded, while slipping the paper into his pocket. "I'm going to keep a close eye on Jamey's movements. Also, I made a few phone calls and discovered the Baptist Memorial Hospital in Oklahoma City released Hopkins a week ago."

The detective raised a brow. "So, you're thinking the little lady is now getting nervous because this Hopkins guy will want his share?"

"That's the impression I'm getting. I sense she's getting jumpy."

Williams scratched his side burn. "Hmm, makes me wonder if this Nick Albergetti isn't somehow connected. Think I'll look into his background a little deeper." Williams put away his glasses and picked up another piece of pizza. "Sounds mighty intriguing. However, you're sitting there with a Cheshire cat grin, so there must be more." His hand stopped in mid air as he started to take a bite. "Hey, aren't you going to eat any of this?"

Hawkman took a piece. "I have a hunch Jamey may plan on selling a diamond."

The detective grimaced. "How? You think there are any jewelry fences around this small burg? They hang out in the big cities where they can get lost. And besides, most of the gems nowadays are marked."

"I'd assume she's aware of that. I figure she might try to pawn one or two."

"You think she's brave enough to do that?"

Hawkman nodded. "She's one spunky little gal."

The detective wiped his hands, then leaned back in his chair. "So you're thinking her story might be on the up and up, but has a slightly different twist? And you believe Hopkins just might come after her?"

"Wouldn't you?"

"Yeah," he nodded. "You think this Hopkins fellow might harm her?"

"Don't know. His record's clean." Hawkman took a bite of pizza, a big swig of beer and thought about what Jamey had said. He calculated that Carl had a big ego, which told him the man could be very dangerous if cornered.

CHAPTER ELEVEN

Carl thought about the doctor's last instructions as he drove west; to gradually lower the sling each week until his arm could comfortably hang by his side without pain. Then he'd be rid of the cumbersome straps around his neck and waist. The long tedious process would definitely try his patience, and he hated not having full rotation of his arm. But, thank God, he was right handed. Trying to use the computer with his left would have frustrated the hell out of him.

He tired quickly, stopped often at rest stops and found motels early in the evening. Each night, he'd pull out the lap top he'd had to purchase before starting the trip and hook up to the room's phone line. He would then search through Jamey's accounts in hopes of finding some clue as to where she'd gone. But he found no change in the accounts; no payments, no change of address on any of her bills and no calls on the phone card. He'd talked with the landlord before leaving the apartment in Oklahoma and the man claimed he didn't even know Jamey had left. Then to make matters more frustrating, Tina hadn't returned his call. It seemed Jamey had disappeared off the face of the earth once she reached Los Angeles. But Carl figured she'd slip up somewhere. She couldn't just vanish without a trace.

❧

The day Nick left, Tina returned from work with mixed emotions. She missed him, yet was glad to have her space back. After fixing a bite to eat, she went into the living room to relax and watch television until she noticed the dirty film on the screen. She got out the dust cloth and went over the whole room. When she reached the corner table where all her pictures were displayed, she spotted an empty space where Jamey's photo had once been. She searched under and around the table, puzzled about its disappearance.

Tina remembered putting the picture back in its place after she'd reminisced to herself over the fun times she'd had with her best friend. No one else but Nick had been in the house. She sat down on the couch, gnawing her lower lip. He'd never shown an interest in Jamey until recently. Especially the other night when he'd asked a bunch of questions. Why?

For the next few hours, Tina couldn't get the missing picture out of her mind. That night she had a nightmare that Nick had left her for Jamey. Yet, that was silly, he'd never met her. And how would he know where she'd gone when she didn't even know?

Tina arose late on Saturday morning, then busied herself with spring cleaning, trying not to let her imagination run wild over the disappearance of the picture. When she opened the coat closet to retrieve a favorite jacket, a picture frame slid from the shelf and crashed to the floor. She picked it up and recognized it to be the one that had held Jamey's photo. Her heart hammered against her rib cage and doubts flooded her thoughts again. The disappearance of the photo made no sense. Why did Nick take it?

She swept up the remnants of glass and in a fit of jealous rage, threw the whole thing into the trash. She'd no more put the broom away than the phone rang. Picking up the receiver, she spoke in a terse voice. "Hello."

"Hello, Tina. This is Carl Hopkins."

♣

Hawkman decided to drop by Curly's on his way home. He had some questions for Ms. Jamey Louise Schyler and hoped Williams hadn't beaten him to the draw. He flipped on the voice activated recorder in his pocket and entered the establishment, where he noticed that most of the after work crowd had already departed. Sauntering over to the bar where Jamey and Curly were preparing for the next wave of customers, he jovially hit his fist on the top. "Okay, let's have some service here."

Jamey glanced up and smiled. "Hi, Hawkman. You know, I forgot to thank you for saving my life today. If you hadn't dropped by, I'd probably be dead."

"You handle a gun quite well. Where'd you learn?"

"Back in Oklahoma. My dad taught me years ago. It's something you never forget."

"Hey, Hawkman," Curly said, stepping up beside Jamey. "Quite a day you've had already. Detective Williams came by earlier and showed me that guy's picture. And he was definitely the man who showed up here a couple of nights ago. All my waitresses went crazy over the new good-looking dude in town." Curly shook his head. "Damn, he looked and acted like a gentleman. Who would have suspected he'd pull that stunt."

Hawkman pointed a finger at him. "How many times do I have to tell you, you can't tell a crook by their looks."

Curly raised his hands in surrender. "I know, I know. You've lectured me a hundred times." He let out a sigh. "So, what brings you in here tonight?"

"I'd like to talk to Jamey if you can spare her for a few minutes."

"Sure," he nodded and waved her from behind the bar. "The crowd won't hit for another thirty or forty minutes."

Hawkman led her out to the far corner of the lighted front patio.

"Why all the secrecy?" she asked.

"Just wanted to ask you some questions in private."

"For instance?"

"Why'd you change your name?"

The color drained from Jamey's face, but she quickly gathered her composure. "What do you mean?"

"If you're Rachel Smith's last living relative like you said, your real name is Jasmine Louise Gray and there's no record of you getting married."

She shrugged. "If you're such a great private eye, you should have figured that one out."

"I'm trying. But you have a driver's license that states you're Jamey Schyler."

She rolled her eyes. "Don't tell me you didn't know that people can get a fake license that looks real for about fifty bucks."

"Yes, I realize that, but it's risky if you're caught with it. You could be thrown in jail."

She sighed. "Listen, I was willing to take the chance so that Carl couldn't find me."

"Why?"

"I already told you the reason."

"What if I don't buy it."

"I'd say, too bad. It's the truth."

Hawkman watched her closely. "Maybe you should give me a description of Hopkins so I can keep an eye out for him."

Jamey stood pondering for a moment, winding a piece of hair around her finger. Then she turned and faced him. "Why are you so interested in my life? Remember, I didn't hire you to protect me."

"No, but I'm a witness to you killing a man and I think that entitles me to some explanation."

She let out a disgusted breath. "Carl is six foot tall, good looking, with sandy brown hair, deep blue eyes, and he's really into computers."

Hawkman frowned. "That describes over half of the Caucasian male race. Could you give me a few more details?"

"What do you want to know?"

"How old is he?"

"Probably in his early thirties. I really don't know."

"Is he thin, fat or medium? Is his hair short or long? What about a tattoo or birthmark? Does he have a beard or mustache? Give me something I'd recognize if I spotted him.

"He's medium weight, short hair, no tattoo or birthmark and no beard or mustache the last time I saw him. And he has a crooked nose. Got it broken in high school basketball." She put both her hands up to her face, making right angles. "His jaw is sort of squared off."

"And he drives a black Tacoma?"

She nodded. "With a big white skinned spot on the right rear side of the tail gate. The idiot backed into a light pole one night and scraped off the paint." Jamey glanced toward several customers entering the bar. "I've got to go."

At home that night after work, Jamey booted up the computer and went online. She'd always been computer savvy, but Carl had taught her much more about the system and she'd been tracking his whereabouts through his credit card bills. He'd left Oklahoma City three days ago, following her same route, indicating that he'd tracked her in the same manner. She caught her breath when she saw his last entry at a motel in Los Angeles. Her paper trail ended there and she hoped it would stop him. But she knew Carl had a stubborn streak. He'd find her, even if it took a year. More than likely, he'd contacted Tina by now. Thank goodness she'd never mentioned Medford to her. She'd have to keep close tabs on Carl's movements from now on. Her stomach contracted when she envisioned the day he'd catch up with her.

Mitzi jumped onto her lap and Jamey ran her hand down the soft fur of the cat's back, making her purr in contentment. "Oh, Mitzi, I don't know what to do," she said, hugging the animal to her chest.

Shutting down the computer, she figured she should get serious about choosing a pawn shop. Her money would run out soon and her salary at Curly's wouldn't cover her expenses.

She'd gone through the phone book and found "Kaufmann's Will Buy It". Their ad stated they'd loan, buy or sell jewelry, gold, diamonds, watches or any other thing you wanted for cash. She'd driven by the shop in the older part of town and found it to be a small place tucked between a hardware store and a Chinese restaurant. It definitely gave the appearance of having been there for eons, which she hoped indicated that they were fair in their prices.

She'd also checked out Johnson's Pawn Shop in the Rogue

Valley Mall and observed that they had everything set up on computers. They'd be able to run the diamond's number through the system and discover it stolen before she got out the door. No, too risky to do business there.

Those two were the only pawn shops for miles around, which limited her choices. And driving to another town really didn't make that much sense. A pawn shop is a pawn shop and they all operated pretty much along the same lines.

Putting the cat down, she stretched and yawned. "Time to go to bed, Mitzi."

The next day, Jamey climbed into her car, took out the bag of diamonds tucked behind the ashtray and removed a one carat stone. She wrapped the gem in a handkerchief, placed it in her purse, then returned the pouch to its hiding place. Driving down the road, she tuned the radio to a rock station, moving her head to the rhythm of the music. She found a parking spot in front of the shop and took a moment to check her lipstick in the mirror. Wanting to appear more sophisticated, she'd braided her long hair into a single French twist, letting wisps of curls frame her oval face. Smiling at her new image, she flipped up the visor and stepped from the car.

When she entered the shop, a small bell tinkled above her head. A musty smell hit her nostrils that reminded her of an antique shop. The lights were dim, and coming inside from a bright sunny day made her squint for a moment before she could focus on the interior. The walls were covered with pictures and hanging trinkets, the shelves loaded with statues of all sizes. Several glass covered cases stood end to end, filled with cameras, video games, guns, calculators, laptop computers and other high priced items. Her gaze fell on a small glass enclosed cabinet that she'd started toward, when a hearty voice spoke out of the stillness, causing her to stop.

"Hello, may I help you?"

She jerked her head to the right and spotted a gray haired man in a short-sleeved white dress shirt sitting at a small desk behind a cluttered counter. An old tweed jacket with leather elbows hung over the back of his chair and a solitary lamp glowed brightly down on the piece of jewelry that seemed to command his full attention. He removed the loupe from his eye and gave her a formal smile.

"I'm looking for the owner," Jamey said.

"Aah, my young lady, you've found him. Kaufmann's been here for many years."

Jamey noted his thick German accent as she continued to survey the premises. She saw nothing modern about this place, which set her mind at ease. Even the cash register operated manually. And there appeared to be no other help around.

She glanced into the glass topped show case directly in front of him. "Oh my, what beautiful jewelry. It all looks antique."

The elderly man finally stood and moved some items off the top so she could get a better view. "These pieces came from the old country. They belonged to my parents and grandparents, who smuggled them out of Germany during the Second World War. I'm really in no hurry to sell them, but if someone offers me the right price, I'll be tempted." He looked into Jamey's face and smiled. "Are you interested? I can tell you the history of each one."

Jamey shook her head. "No, I'm afraid I couldn't afford them. I've really come to talk to you about..."

But before she could finish her sentence, his crooked, arthritic fingers had removed a large brooch from the case and put it on a piece of black velvet in front of her.

"This belonged to my grandmother and is the piece that enabled me to get started in America."

He launched into a tale about the woman and Jamey started losing her patience. "Mr. Kaufmann, I really need to talk to you about some business because I have to go to work soon."

Glancing up, his eyes had a faraway look as if he'd been reliving the story. "Of course, forgive me. I sometimes get carried away." He quickly replaced the pin and limped around the counter with a piece of paper in his hand. "Please fill out my customer form."

To appease him, Jamey quickly scribbled in the information and handed it back.

"Now what can I do for you, Ms...?" he shoved on the glasses that hung around his neck on a thin braided rope.

"Schyler," she said before he had a chance to read her name. "Do you buy loose diamonds?"

His small beady eyes glistened. "Oh yes, I buy almost any kind of gems if they're of good quality. Do you have something you'd like to sell?"

"Yes, but I'm not quite ready to part with it, but thought I'd ask you about it first." She glanced around the room. "Don't you have a private office that we can go into?"

He waved an arm. "This is it. My working area is at that small desk." He chuckled and moved past her toward the front door. "But I'll make you more comfortable." He turned the lock, flipped the hanging sign around to 'closed' and pulled down the window shade that covered the glass door. "How's that?"

It made her a bit nervous to be locked in the room with this man, but she nodded, as he looked harmless.

His back slightly hunched, he hobbled back around behind the counter and put out his hand. "Now, Ms. Schyler, show me what you have."

Jamey nervously fished out the handkerchief from her purse and handed it to him. Biting her lower lip, she watched as he sat down at his desk, carefully unwrapped the diamond and put the loupe to his eye. He studied it for what seemed like an eternity before he pushed the hanky aside and placed the gem on a piece of black velvet cloth.

He stared at her and spoke softly. "I'm surprised you want to sell such a beautiful stone. I assume you'd much rather have it made into a ring or pendant."

Jamey winced at his gaze. "I know it's lovely. It belonged to my grandmother."

He shook his head. "How well I understand." A slight tic twitched at his jaw line. "I told you only part of the story about the brooch. It belonged to my grandmother and I had to sell it to start the business. Many years later I tracked the people down and bought it back. However, with a diamond you might not be so lucky."

"Mr. Kaufmann, I don't mean to be rude, but I have to leave. What would you give me for this stone?"

"I can only offer four hundred dollars. Since a jeweler will have to mount it and make it into a salable piece." He held it up between forefinger and thumb. "Ah, I can already visualize the beautiful ring this would make."

Not wanting to get into any more detailed stories or descriptions, Jamey quickly responded with a counter offer. "Eight hundred. You know that diamond is worth much more."

He eyed her suspiciously. "You're sure it's not stolen."

Feeling her stomach jerk, she put a hand on her hip. "Now that would be pretty dumb to come in here and try to pawn off one stolen diamond."

He nodded. "Others have tried it." Then he gazed into her face. "Five hundred."

"Six hundred, otherwise I'll have to go elsewhere." Jamey said, holding out her hand.

He let out a dry chuckle as he placed the diamond in her palm. "You drive a hard bargain young lady, but you're right. It's a beauty of a gem. So when do you think you'll be coming back?" he asked, handing her the handkerchief.

"Not sure, maybe in a couple of weeks. At least, I know you're interested."

Kaufmann unlocked the door and Jamey left. She hopped into her car and took several deep breaths. The man seemed lonely and would have blabbed all day if she hadn't hurried him along. But he seemed fair on his price. He offered more than she expected.

A loud sigh erupted from her lips as she started the car. Her thoughts went back to Hawkman's questions last night. He seemed as adept with the computer as Carl and she wondered how much he already knew. She had the feeling he could back her into a corner if she wasn't careful.

Deep in thought about what Hawkman might have uncovered, she drove back to the cottage. Suddenly, she shivered outwardly, as again that pesky cold chill slid down her spine.

CHAPTER TWELVE

Ludwig Kaufmann flipped up the shade on the door, then stood for a moment watching Jamey as she backed out of the parking space and drove down the street. Once she disappeared from sight, he returned to his desk, rubbing his hands together. He didn't quite buy the story that she'd inherited that beautiful diamond from her grandmother, as marking gems didn't come into practice until about ten years ago. However, he mustn't rush to judgment. Nowadays grandparents had more money and were passing valuable items down to their heirs before they died, instead of writing them into a will. So, her story could be plausible.

But to be on the safe side, he ruffled through a stack of papers until he found the roster of stolen gems sent out by the insurance companies twice a year. He checked the number he'd jotted down against the list and found no match. Relieved, he sat back and smacked his lips. That diamond would make him a nice little profit from the right buyer. He wondered if she had any more of the same quality.

As Jamey approached her place, her heart skipped a beat when she recognized Hawkman's truck parked in the shade of the big oak tree. "What the hell's he doing here?" she mumbled. "The snoop has probably found out something else."

It looked as if he'd fallen asleep. His head was thrown back with his hat pulled down over his eyes, a toothpick dangled from the corner of his mouth.

Jamey parked under the tarp next to the house, slammed

the car door, then marched up to his truck and slapped the side with the palm of her hand. "Hawkman, what are you doing here?"

He raised up and adjusted the brim of his hat. "Hello, Ms. Schyler. I didn't finish my talk with you yesterday, so thought I'd stop by."

She scowled. "Would you please drop the Ms. Schyler bit and call me Jamey. You make me sound like a damned old lady."

He chuckled. "Okay, Jamey."

"So, how much more do you have to say? If it's going to take awhile, you might as well come inside. I don't cherish the thought of standing beside this truck and looking up at you until I get a crick in my neck."

Hawkman followed her inside and sat down in the living room.

"You want a soda?" she called from the kitchen.

"Sure."

Jamey carried in two ice filled glasses, brimming with Coke. She handed one to Hawkman, then sat down on the sofa. "Okay, start talking."

He came forward in his seat and took a swallow of the drink. "I've been thinking over the story you told me about Carl Hopkins. Is he wealthy?"

Jamey hooted and shook her head. "Hell, no. What gave you that idea?"

"I just can't figure a man chasing a woman clear across the country, especially when he doesn't know where she's headed. The west coast is a big place. Now if money were no object, that's different."

She glared at him. "You can believe what you want, Hawkman. But I know Carl and you don't."

Hawkman exhaled loudly and looked straight into her eyes. "Jamey, get off it. Drop this cock and bull story. Tell me the truth."

She fidgeted with her glass and wouldn't meet his stare.

He leaned closer, never taking his gaze from her face. "I know that Carl Hopkins had a confrontation with a diamond courier at the Regency Hotel in Oklahoma City. Hopkins received gun shot wounds and was released from the hospital two weeks ago. The police report included the statement from the hotel clerk, who described a young woman who'd accompanied Carl to his room on the evening in question. The description fits you."

She jumped up, her eyes narrowed into slits. "That's a damn lie."

He raised a hand. "Sit down, Jamey. I'm not through."

She dropped to the edge of the couch, her spine rigid. "Go on," she demanded.

"Isn't it true that Hopkins moved into your apartment about six months ago? It appears he used his salary to pay the rent along with most of the bills. I also found out where you both used to work. And I found it quite interesting that you were employed at a jewelry store." He hesitated and raised a brow. "Young lady, you could be in a heap of trouble."

With her eyes flickering like hot coals, she snapped, "You've done a hell of a lot of snooping without getting paid. Why would I be in trouble? Because I want a man out of my life? We had a little fling going and before I knew it, without any invitation from me, he'd moved into my apartment. After a short time, he got real possessive. I didn't know how to get out of the relationship without a scene. So when that hotel mess happened and he went into the hospital, I saw my chance."

"Were you at the hotel with him?"

She nodded. "He made me go."

"Then you knew he planned on stealing the diamonds?"

"Not really. He talked about it, but I didn't think he'd go through with it. I'd warned him that some of these couriers carried guns, but he wouldn't listen."

"So you were there the whole time?"

"No. When he staggered back into the room with blood all over him, he told me to get out." She shrugged. "So I ran down the fire escape stairs and left."

"He didn't give you any diamonds to hold?"

"Good Lord, no," she said, emphatically. "I wouldn't have

taken them if he'd offered." Raising a brow, she glanced at Hawkman. "I thought the paper stated they didn't find any on him or in the room."

"Yes, I read the articles. That's why I asked."

She hooked a thumb toward her chest. "Oh my God. You think I have the diamonds?" Then she pointed at him. "The only mistake I made was using the damn credit cards he gave me."

"How's that?"

"He's a computer hacker and could follow my electronic trail. When it dawned on me what I'd done, I destroyed the cards in Los Angeles, hoping he'd give up when he couldn't track me any farther. Now I'm following his trek using my laptop, so I'll be able to figure out how close he's getting."

"If you don't have the diamonds, why is he after you? Do you owe him money?"

She shook her head violently. "No, no. He just wants me back."

"I can't believe that."

Jerking up her head, she glared at him. "Because he's in love with me and very jealous. He'd kill before he let anyone else have me."

Hawkman's set his empty glass on the end table. "Jamey, I hate to disappoint you, but I don't buy it. You have something he wants mighty bad, or you owe him a big hunk of money."

She arose from her seat and moved so close to his face that their noses almost touched. "Obviously, you've never been in love, Mr. Hawkman. Well, you can take it or leave it, but that's the damn truth."

He leaned back and returned her stare. "I definitely don't want to see you hurt, Jamey. You indicated that Carl would kill. Is he that dangerous? Has he ever hurt you?"

She shook her head. "No. But he has an uncanny way of making a person do things. That's what scares me. He's going to be awfully mad because I left, and I'm not sure what he'll do."

"What if he finds you and Mark together? If he's as possessive as you say, would Mark be in jeopardy?"

She wrinkled her forehead. "I'm not sure."

Hawkman slammed his hands down on the arm rest, making her jump.

"Dammit, Jamey, level with me! One minute you say he wouldn't hurt anyone, the next minute you say he would. What the hell's going on?"

Turning away, she hugged her waist. "I can't tell you any more. It's too personal."

He exhaled loudly through his tight lips. "Keep me informed of Carl's movements. If you happen to spot him in town, call me immediately." He wrote his cell phone number on the back of one of his business cards and handed it to her. "You can reach me here night or day."

Hawkman stormed out of the house. The woman frustrated the hell out of him. He certainly didn't want her hurt, but he didn't know whether he could believe a word she uttered. There was something very screwy here, he thought, climbing into the cab of his truck. He made a U-turn and gunned down the road heading toward his office.

Later that day as he sat at his desk, Hawkman rubbed a hand across his face. He couldn't get Jamey off his mind. Getting up, he dumped his cold coffee, poured a fresh cup and crossed over to the window. Detective Williams still hadn't heard from the Los Angeles Police Department about Nick Albergetti. Hawkman agreed with Williams that they couldn't put him in the picture yet, but the man must have been after the diamonds. But how would he have known about the gems or that Jamey had them?

Williams had run a check on Jamey's phone and discovered she'd only received one long distant phone call from Oklahoma which turned out to be from a pay phone. Curious, but it didn't give much of a clue.

Staring into space, Hawkman decided to put a tail on the girl. He needed to find out where she went during the day. But who could he use that wouldn't cost an arm and a leg? Then a smile curled his lips. He crossed the room, picked up the phone and punched a memory button. "Hello, Jennifer. I'm going to need your help."

After explaining the situation, he worked out a schedule. He'd watch Jamey in the evening, since she didn't leave Curly's until after midnight. Then Jennifer would come in about ten in the morning while he grabbed a few winks of sleep. There would be a few hours where no one had her under observation, but Hawkman figured he'd take that chance since Jamey usually slept in, not starting her day until near noon. He felt pretty confident about the surveillance arrangement.

After Hawkman left, Jamey felt like she'd been dragged over hot embers. The mention of Mark being in danger made her anxious. She didn't want anything to happen to him. "Damn!" she muttered. "I knew I shouldn't have led him on. Especially, since he knows nothing about Carl."

She had an hour and a half before work time, so she decided to run to the post office. Sorting through the junk mail, she smiled when she spotted the expected letter. She flipped the rest of the junk mail into the trash bin and hurried back to the car.

When she returned to the cottage and read the letter, she frowned. Things were moving too slowly. This bothered her. She went into the kitchen over the sink and set the letter afire, watching it as it turned to ashes. She scraped up the charred pieces and took them into the bathroom where she flushed them down the toilet.

Lugging the laptop from the closet, she set it on table and booted it up. She checked Carl's whereabouts and breathed a sigh of relief to see he hadn't left Los Angeles. Shutting down, she returned the computer to its hiding place. After changing into a clean uniform, she stood for a moment gazing out the window. It wouldn't be long before she'd have to go see Mr. Kaufmann. Her money wouldn't hold out too much longer.

She checked her watch. Thirty minutes until work time. She'd go in early. It made the night pass more quickly and Curly always seemed to appreciate her help. He'd even told her how pretty she looked with her new hair style. She'd noticed her tips had gone up, but that could have been due to the new sexy outfits Curly had bought for the waitresses: low-cut tight tops with short skirts. She smiled to herself at Mark's jealous reaction the first night she wore one. He must have hated the sight of her bouncing around with her boobs half hanging out so all the men could ogle. Curly paid his help well and had the best looking cocktail waitresses in town, but Mark didn't particularly like the idea of his woman being one of them.

"His woman," she grumbled, checking her lipstick in the mirror one more time before picking up her purse and heading out the door. "Not for long, my dear boy."

As she drove toward work, she wondered what Hawkman had in mind. He seemed much too interested in her, and she didn't like the idea of his snooping so much. Of course, she'd given him the impression that Carl was jealous and possibly dangerous. But what did she really know about Carl? Not much, she resolved. Especially after seeing him work the heist with those brass knuckles. Hawkman could be right; Mark's life might be in jeopardy. The thought made her shudder.

CHAPTER THIRTEEN

Not wanting to disturb her husband, Jennifer slipped quietly out of bed. She'd felt him crawl in beside her early this Sunday morning. Curly kept the bar open late on Friday and Saturday nights and she knew Hawkman would hang around until Jamey arrived home safely.

She dressed, ate a bowl of cold cereal and left the house around nine. When she arrived at Jamey's address, she drove around the block to familiarize herself with the area. Hawkman had described the girl's car and she spotted the Toyota parked under a make-shift tarp carport near the back door. Jennifer noted the time at ten o'clock, yet there were still no visible signs of life. She hunted for a good place to park and finally discovered a tree covered area near the creek about a half block away. Backing into the shade of a large oak, she had full view of the house and Jamey's car.

Jennifer had done surveillance for Hawkman many times and knew it could be quite boring. She'd come prepared with a pad for jotting down notes as some of this information could benefit her mystery series. Also, she had her Palm reader tucked in her purse, loaded with several books.

Using her binoculars, Jennifer cased the house from front to back. Thirty minutes elapsed before the curtains in one of the rooms were pulled back. A young woman stood at the window looking out for several moments before turning away. Jennifer had never met Jamey, but recognized her from Hawkman's description. Unfortunately, she couldn't see that sexy belly button ring.

Shortly, Jamey came out the back door, and headed straight

for her car. Jennifer quickly shifted her stuff to the passenger seat and prepared to follow. She didn't have to worry about Jamey recognizing her if she got too close, because Hawkman never displayed family photos in his office. She let the Toyota get about a half block away before starting the mini van.

Tailing Jamey into the older part of town, Jennifer watched her park in front of Kaufmann's pawn shop. If Hawkman's theory proved right, the girl would try to pawn a diamond. Jennifer took a parking space three cars down from the store entrance. She decided to stay in her vehicle, not wanting to risk the chance that Ludwig Kaufmann might recognize her if she strolled by the shop. Within a few minutes Jamey stormed out of the door in an agitated state and headed straight for her car.

Jennifer recognized the pawn shop owner as he followed Jamey out onto the sidewalk with his hands extended in a pleading manner. She quickly rolled down her window and heard him say, "Ms. Schyler, I'm sure we can work something out."

"You're just trying to cheat me," Jamey spat, jumping into her car and gunning her engine. She backed out and headed down the street.

Jennifer quickly dialed Hawkman as she started the van and hurried in pursuit. When he answered, she related the incident. "She didn't seem to be a happy camper. What do you think it means? Does this make any sense to you?"

"Yes. I'll explain what I think has happened later. You've done a great job, hon. Where's she heading?"

"She's traveling toward her house. I thought about following her inside the shop, but feared Ludwig might recognize me."

Hawkman laughed. "Well, try not to blow your cover for at least a day or two. I'm going to make some calls, then I'll relieve you in a couple of hours."

"No problem. See ya later."

She slipped the cell phone into her shirt pocket and proceeded through the traffic, keeping the Toyota in sight. After Jamey stopped at the dry cleaners, she returned to the cottage and Jennifer again parked under the oak tree.

As the day went by, the warm weather heated up the interior of the van and Jennifer found herself becoming drowsy and snapped her eyelids open to stay awake. Finally, she slipped on a pair of over-sized sunglasses, grabbed the clipboard and climbed out of the van. Looking like someone taking a survey, she decided a quick walk around the block would help keep her alert.

When she turned the corner and headed toward her vehicle, she noticed a strange old pick-up had parked next to her van. The sun glared off the windshield and she couldn't see the occupant, so she approached with caution. Then a very familiar voice asked, "Where were you?"

"Hawkman! For crying out loud, where'd you get that truck?"

He laughed. "This is Stan's old junker that he uses to haul stuff. I'm borrowing it for a couple of days and left mine at his place. Jamey would recognize the 4X4."

"How long do you think you can keep it a secret that we're watching her? You know she'll recognize you immediately."

"I've brought a couple of disguises with me. I'll slap on a baseball cap and my Ray Ban sunglasses to hide the patch. I'm only going to do this for a couple of days, as I think she's already made her move by going to the pawn shop. It won't be long before we know for sure she has the diamonds. Remind me to talk to Williams about having a talk with Ludwig Kaufmann soon."

"I'll try to remember, but you better write yourself a note." Jennifer stepped back and eyed the old vehicle. "Well, I certainly hope you don't have to take on a chase. You'll come out the loser."

"The outside fools you. Stan has a hunker of an engine in this little babe."

She smiled. "That doesn't surprise me." Getting into her van, she rolled down the window. "I'll take off now. See you in the morning.

"Thanks for a good job," he said, giving her a little salute.

Jennifer waved as she pulled onto the road and grinned to

herself as she noted Hawkman adjusting the seat to make room for his long legs.

❧

Carl sat on the edge of the bed in his Los Angeles motel room and stared at the picture of Jamey he'd placed in his wallet. It had been over a week since he'd called Tina, and still no word. He thought he'd made some headway when he pleaded with her to help him find Jamey, especially after he gave her the old 'how much I love her, can't live without her' line. Tina had promised that she'd call him on his cell phone the minute she heard from Jamey.

He sighed and closed his billfold, then went to the table and booted up the laptop. Running through the credit card statements again, he hoped to see some activity, but found none. She'd obviously discarded them.

Thinking there was a possibility that she might have traded in her car, he used his DOS knowledge as a hacker, and entered the registration area of the California Department of Motor Vehicles. After about an hour of reviewing the site, he sat back and frowned at the monitor. Nothing.

He'd just about come to the conclusion that he might as well wrap it up as a lost cause, when his cell phone rang. Knowing it had to be from either Tina or Jamey, he frantically yanked it from his pocket.

"Hello."

"Carl this is Tina."

He clutched the phone tightly to his ear. "Have you heard anything?"

Her voice broke. "Yes, but I think you better come over. I can't tell you over the phone."

"I'll be there in fifteen minutes. Give me instructions on how to get to your place." Carl, fearing something had happened to Jamey, leaped into his car within three minutes of hanging up from Tina.

❧

Jamey stepped out of the shower, still fuming from her encounter with Mr. Kaufmann, when she heard the phone ringing. She grabbed a towel and wrapped it around her naked body as she hurried into the kitchen. "Hello."

"Ms. Schyler?"

"Speaking."

"This is Ludwig Kaufmann at the pawn shop. I'm sorry I upset you. Surely we can work out some agreement on the diamond."

Recognizing the heavy German accent, she regretted filling out the customer card listing her real phone number and address. "Look, Mr. Kaufmann, don't call me anymore unless you give me what you promised on my first visit. Don't try and cheat me. That diamond doesn't have a flaw. I know what it's worth."

Kaufmann cleared his throat. "I tell you what. Why don't you stop by and let me look at it again. I'm sure we can come to some sort of an arrangement."

"I can't today, I'm on my way to work."

"I see. What's your work schedule? I can always meet you here at the store after hours."

Jamey hesitated, not liking the sound of his suggestion. "I have different hours each day. I'll give you a call when I'm free."

He paused. "Do you have any spare time tomorrow?"

"Maybe. I'll let you know."

She hung up and stared at the phone. The man unnerved her. But she didn't know where else to turn. The way he'd looked at her after examining the diamond through that loupe gave her the creeps. He had a sleazy phony smile and cold eyes. It frightened her that he might have recognized the diamond's marking as one stolen. If so, why hadn't he called the cops? She shivered at the thought as she hurried back to the bathroom to get dressed.

To hell with calling him. He doesn't need to know what hours I work. And I'll be more vigilant of people hanging around here. He might send someone to watch me. She raked a hand through her hair and looked in the mirror. "Don't get paranoid," she spoke aloud to her reflection. "Otherwise, you'll make a mistake."

Jamey made up her mind that if she offered him another diamond, one of the larger ones, she wouldn't take a penny less than a thousand dollars.

❧

Hawkman checked his watch and glanced at the cottage. He figured he had nearly an hour to wait before Jamey left for work, so he pulled his phone from his pocket and keyed in Detective Williams' number, hoping to catch him at his desk.

"Hey, Williams, Hawkman here. Don't they ever let you out of that office anymore?"

"Hell no," he laughed. "Everything has to have my signature on it or it won't get past the big boys. What can I do for you?"

"Wondering if you could tell me anything about Ludwig Kaufmann, the pawn shop owner in the old part of town."

"Kaufmann's Pawn Shop," he repeated. "Been there for years. Never had a complaint against him. He minds his own business and does his job. And, exceptionally well from what I understand. Most people come away from there quite happy."

"Sounds like he's successful and legal."

"Why'd you ask?"

"Jamey made a visit to his shop."

"Ah, ha! That's interesting. We may have to pay him a visit. Say, while I've got you on the line, I had a call from the Los Angeles Police Department on Nick Albergetti."

"Oh yeah? Anything to sink our teeth into?"

"Not sure yet. He's a small time con man, but active. A snitch down south gave the information that he spent a lot of his time with a lady named Tina Randolph. The police located the woman and presented her with the news of Nick's death occurring here in Medford. She asked them what had happened and they told her he'd been shot by the victim, Jamey Schyler, whom he'd tried to terrorize."

"What was her reaction?"

"Don't know. They didn't comment about that."

"I might have to ask Jamey about this Tina. What was her last name?"

"Randolph."

Hawkman slipped the cellular back into his pocket just as Jamey came out of the house. At that moment, Mark drove around the corner and pulled in next to her car.

He jumped out and tried to give Jamey a kiss, but she stepped back holding her nose and pointed at his filthy jeans and shirt. It appeared to Hawkman, that Mark had been working in a field or at a gas station. The two love birds chatted for a moment, then Jamey got into her car, Mark into his, and they left the premises going in opposite directions. Hawkman adjusted the brim on the baseball hat, bringing it down close to the top of his sun glasses and pulled away from the shade of the oak tree. However, Jamey's next move puzzled him. She didn't head for work, but circled back toward the older part of town. He followed at a distance and was intrigued when she stopped at the pawn shop again.

CHAPTER FOURTEEN

Carl stood outside Tina's apartment, shifting from foot to foot as he waited for her to answer the bell. He'd never met the woman before, but had seen an old picture and noted her striking looks. The photo in no way prepared him for the dark haired, green eyed beauty who opened the door. Maturity had done this female a favor. She didn't have the natural beauty that Jamey possessed, but her soft aura caught Carl off guard. "Uh, hello, I'm Carl Hopkins."

She stepped back and held the door ajar for him to enter. "Please come in."

Carl moved inside and she gestured toward the couch. "Make yourself comfortable. Can I get you a soda or beer?"

A beer sounded great, but afraid of giving the wrong impression, he said, "A soda's fine."

Once they were both seated in the living room, Carl felt a bit awkward, unsure of how to start the conversation. "You said you had some news about Jamey."

Tina looked him square in the face. "Yes, she shot and killed my lover."

Carl almost dropped his glass. "What?"

She raised a hand. "I'm sorry, that sounded rather abrupt. The police called it self-defense. Nick must have threatened her. But what I find bizarre, is that they didn't even know each other."

Carl slid to the edge of the seat. "You're going to have to back up, I'm not following. Did this happen in Los Angeles?"

"No. Medford, Oregon."

He frowned. "Medford?"

"Yes."

"Are you sure it was Jamey Gray that shot him?"

"The police called her Jamey Schyler. At first, the name didn't register. Then it hit me like a bomb."

"How so?

"The Schylers are the people who took Jamey into their home after her parents were killed."

"But why would she change her name?"

"Obviously, because of you."

Carl nodded. "Yeah, I guess that makes sense." Then he frowned. "How did your boyfriend find her?"

Tina gnawed her lower lip and shook her head. "I don't have the foggiest notion. They'd never met. And she didn't even know his name. It's driving me crazy."

"Be candid with me, Tina. You truly didn't know Jamey had gone to Oregon?"

She looked bewildered and wide-eyed. "No. The last thing Jamey said was that she'd let me know where she settled after her trip to Mexico. I haven't heard from her since."

Carl rubbed a hand over his chin. "I had a sneaking suspicion she never went to Mexico." He took a deep breath. "Tell me about your beau and why you think he tracked her down?"

Tina stood and hugged herself as she paced. She launched into telling Carl about Nick Albergetti, the con man who would go after a dime if he thought he had a chance of getting it. "I know how he thought. And after I told Nick about you being involved in a diamond heist, he asked me a lot of questions."

Carl raised his brows. "Jamey told you about that venture?"

Tina flopped down on the couch and sighed. "I'm sure she only told me the parts she wanted me to know."

"Did she tell you about her involvement?"

She glanced at him in shock. "No."

Early the next morning, Jamey rolled over and opened her eyes. "Mark, why are you up? She squinted at the clock and groaned. "Oh, hell, it's only seven o'clock."

"I promised old man Carson I'd help him finish cleaning his barn today. We almost wrapped it up yesterday, but he got awfully tired and I didn't think it the healthiest work for him to continue."

"Your clothes smelled like cow manure. So be sure you go home, shower and change before coming over here."

Mark laughed. "Well, since animals are a big part of what's in a barn, I'd say that makes sense. I promise I'll smell sweet as new mown hay when I return."

After he left, Jamey drifted back to sleep and didn't crawl out of bed until noon. She threw on her robe, grabbed her hair brush off the bathroom sink and ran it through her hair as she headed for the kitchen to put on a fresh pot of coffee. Dragging the lap top out of the closet, she booted it up and stared at the monitor as it went through its steps. She keyed in Carl's credit card number, then scrolled down to the last few entries. "Dear God," she mumbled, dropping into the chair, her heart racing. "He's checked out of the motel and gassed up his car. It will be hours before I know in which direction he's headed."

She sat for several minutes, her eyes fixed on the screen. Finally, she shut down the computer and paced. If he heads north out of Los Angeles, I'll know he's found me. But how? I changed my name, haven't used a credit card, don't have a checking account and paid cash for everything. Stay calm, she thought, he could be heading back to Oklahoma.

Regardless, she'd better go talk to Kaufmann again and offer him another diamond. She poured a cup of coffee and headed for the bathroom to get dressed. Her hands shook as she French braided her hair, then burned her finger with the curling iron as she twirled the tendrils around her face. "Damn," she yelped, sucking on her finger.

Dashing out of the house, she jumped into her car. She'd purposely hid the bag of bigger diamonds behind the front ashtray and quickly extracted one. Folding it into a handkerchief, she stuffed the pouch back into its hiding place. When she pulled into the street, she noticed a silver gray mini van parked near the creek, but didn't think much about it.

She reached the post office and found only junk mail in her box. Disgusted, she dumped it all into the trash can, hurried back to the car and drove toward the older part of town via the back streets. Her nerves tingled as she felt time squashing her under its heels.

When she entered the pawn shop, Kaufmann had a customer, so Jamey stood and stared out the window. Even though she knew Carl couldn't possibly be here yet, she nervously fiddled with the strap of her purse and automatically checked the parking lot for a black Tacoma Toyota.

Finally, the person left and Kaufmann waved for her to come to the counter. "Ah, Ms. Schyler. What can I do for you? I hope you brought me another diamond."

Did he know something? Jamey felt her heart squeeze in fear. "First, I want to ask a question."

He glanced at her with a puzzled expression. "Yes?"

"Does the mark on the diamond make it less valuable?"

"Quite the contrary," he said, smiling. "It informs the jeweler where the gem originated and tells us its quality. Nowadays most of the big companies have their trademarks etched in the stones."

She pulled the handkerchief from her purse and handed him the gem. Holding her breath, she watched him twist and turn it between his fingers. Then he placed the jewel on a piece of black velvet and adjusted the loupe to his eye. Finally, he looked up.

"I apologize for taking so long. This diamond is beautiful. It also has the company's mark as did the last one. I can give you seven hundred for this stone."

Jamey clenched her hands together to keep her composure. "I want a thousand. You know it's worth it."

"Yes, but you realize I have to set it into a ring or pendant and that'll cost me. To make some sort of profit, the most I can offer you is eight hundred and fifty."

She gritted her teeth. "Mr. Kaufmann, we both know that diamond is worth three times what I want for it. If you won't pay me a thousand dollars, I'll find someone else."

He held up his hand. "You do drive a hard bargain, Ms. Schyler. Let me check and see if I have enough cash on hand." He dropped down on his haunches and twisted the dial on his safe under the desk.

Jamey felt beads of sweat pop out on her forehead and quickly dabbed at them with the handkerchief she'd wrapped around the diamond. She knew that before long the marks on the stones would be listed as stolen. The thought made her insides jerk. Within a few moments, Kaufmann stood with a handful of bills.

"You're in luck, Ms. Schyler. I have enough to pay you."

He counted out ten one hundred dollar bills into her palm, then he looked into her eyes with a steely gray stare. "Now, I have some questions. What are you going to do with all that money? And where did you get these lovely gems?"

She returned his glare. "Mr. Kaufmann. I don't think what I do with my money is any of your business. And I've already told you the stones came from my grandmother."

His gaze never left her eyes. "As long as they weren't stolen."

She yanked her hand away, clutching the bills. "How dare you insinuate such a thing."

Wrapping the diamond in the velvet, he shrugged and bent over to place the gem inside the safe. "I have to protect myself."

Jamey tucked the money into her purse and headed for the door. Her hand on the knob, she turned and faced him. "Thank you, Mr. Kaufmann. It was a pleasure doing business with you," she lied.

His mouth formed that horrid smile. "Please keep me in mind for any future sales."

"I will," she said, and walked out the door. Her heart pounded as she wondered if she'd be out of the area in less than thirty days. That's all the time she'd probably have until discovery.

❧

Jennifer watched as Jamey dashed out the front door of the cottage. The girl had that look of panic on her face and turned her head from side to side, as if looking for someone. Wondering what had upset her, Jennifer scanned the area, but didn't see anything out of the ordinary. Puzzled, she started the van and followed the Toyota through the back streets. Where was the girl going?

First, Jamey stopped at the post office, but returned to her car in a matter of seconds, still looking quite disgruntled. Jennifer continued behind her as they circled through the back streets and eventually came out in the older part of town. Jamey parked in front of Kaufmann's and hurried inside. Thinking her behavior quite peculiar, Jennifer called Hawkman.

"Jamey's acting mighty strange. More like frightened." She described her actions to Hawkman, but only received silence on the other end of the phone. "Did I lose you?" Jennifer asked.

"No, I'm still here, just thinking. Are you still at the pawn shop?

"Yes."

"I'm almost to Medford. Keep me informed of her whereabouts."

"Okay."

After thirty minutes, Jennifer began to get concerned as to why Jamey had not come out of the shop. Just as she decided to walk past the place and glimpse in the window, the girl stepped out of the building. Her body language gave Jennifer the impression of agitation as she dropped her purse, snatched it up, then fumbled inside for her keys as she walked toward her car. Jamey again nervously glanced around the parking lot, her gaze hesitated for a moment on the van. She then jumped into her car and drove toward the residential area. Jennifer punched redial on her phone as she headed out behind the Toyota.

"Hawkman, I'll have to keep you informed where we come

out of this maze. But I have a feeling we're going back to her place the long way. Right now we're in the midst of cul-de-sacs and side streets. To be honest, I think I'm lost."

"Has she been in the pawn shop all this time?"

"Yes. I started getting worried."

"That's interesting. I'm going to drop by the police station."

"Why?"

"I think it's time Williams and I had a chat with Mr. Ludwig Kaufmann."

CHAPTER FIFTEEN

Hawkman poked his head around the door jamb of Williams' office. The detective sat behind his desk, mumbling something about the damn paperwork as he signed sheet after sheet. When he raised his head to plop a stack into the out basket, he spotted Hawkman.

"Hey, what the devil are you doing standing there with that silly grin spread across your face?"

"I enjoy seeing a man doing what he loves."

"Like hell. You're just thankful you don't have my job. You're out in the field doing what you were born to do." He waved Hawkman in. "Sit your ass down and give me a break."

Hawkman scooted a chair to the front of the desk.

Williams raised a brow. "Okay, What's going on? I know you wouldn't be here otherwise."

"Jamey made another trip to the pawn shop this morning. Think I'll pay Mr. Ludwig Kaufmann a visit."

"Think you'll get any answers?"

He shrugged. "Hard to say, unless I have an arm of the law at my side. But thought it might be worth checking since Jennifer said the girl's acting mighty strange."

"So, now you've got Jennifer working on it?"

Hawkman grinned. "I have to keep my expenses down since I'm not getting paid."

Williams laughed. "Yep. See your point."

"Think you could meet me at the pawn shop in about an hour?"

The detective shook his head and slapped a hand on a stack of papers. "You know I'd jump at the chance if I thought we had anything substantial. Legally, I haven't even heard about the diamond heist yet. All I know is what you've told me. If something shows up, just give me a call. I'll be right here trying to catch up on this mess."

"Well, I certainly don't want to keep you from your duties." Hawkman chuckled and headed out the door.

Before going to Kaufmann's, he decided to drop by Jamey's house and see if she knew this Tina Randolph. But first he stopped by Stan's and picked up his 4X4. No sense in giving his disguise away just yet. He called Jennifer on the cell. "I'm coming over in my own truck, as I want to talk to Jamey. Then I'm heading over to the pawn shop. Can you hang on a little while longer?"

"Sure. But you realize this is only going to delay my writing time. And we might have to add another week before we can head down south."

"Yeah, I know, but this Jamey thing is getting more complicated each day."

He turned the corner and spotted Jennifer's van under the oak tree. Pulling around to the rear of the cottage, he parked next to Jamey's car and went to the back door. After standing there for several moments, Jamey finally opened it a few inches and peeked out. "Thank God, it's you," she said, letting out a breath of relief and throwing open the door. "But what are you doing here?"

"I came to ask a question, but it appears you've got a problem," he said, stepping into the kitchen.

"I'm not sure. Come on into the living room."

He sat down on the worn overstuffed chair in the corner. "You want to tell me?"

Wringing her hands, Jamey paced in front of him. "Carl checked out of his motel in Los Angeles this morning and he's heading north."

"Are you sure?"

"Yes. I've tracked him on the computer and he filled up with gas on Interstate 5 at Kettleman City. He's definitely not heading back to Oklahoma. I have this feeling that he's found me and I can't figure out how."

Hawkman studied the girl as she talked. She actually looked frightened. "Is there anyone in the Los Angeles area that knows your whereabouts?"

"I have a friend living there, but she doesn't know where I am."

"Is her name Tina Randolph?"

Jamey whirled around, her face pale. "How did you know?" she whispered.

"That's why I'm here. I wanted to know if you knew her. The police have connected her to Nick Albergetti."

Jamey covered her face with her hands and dropped to the couch. "Oh my God!"

"Detective Williams just received the information. The police have contacted Tina about Albergetti's death and questioned her. She's innocent of any wrong doing, but she now knows you're here as they told her who shot him."

"It's all making sense now," Jamey said in a harsh voice. "I'm almost positive Tina told Carl."

"How's that?"

"He's never met her personally, but knows she's my best friend from high school. We kept in close contact. If he didn't find her phone number or address back at the apartment, he'd go into the computer." She wrung her hands. "And Tina can't keep a secret even if her life depends on it, so I'm sure she poured out the whole story, especially if Carl fed her a line."

"If Nick Albergetti was Tina's boyfriend, how come you didn't recognize him?"

"That's one secret she kept. She never told me his name and only gave vague information. I just assumed he was a married man and didn't want his identity exposed, so I didn't question her any further."

Hawkman leaned forward, resting his elbows on his thighs. "Back to Carl. If you'd stop playing games and tell me what the man really wants, we might be able to stop him."

Jamey stood, straightened her arms against her sides and clenched her hands into fists. "I've already told you, It's private," she growled.

"And what did I tell you about that story?"

"That you didn't buy it."

"You got that right. If you don't level with me, you're going to end up taking some unnecessary risks and could get hurt."

Her brown eyes were fiery. "I've told you enough."

"Then why have you visited Kaufmann's Pawn Shop several times?"

Her head whipped around and she glared at him. "What the hell is that to you? That has nothing to do with Carl and it's not any of your business. Have you been following me? "

"Hey, I'm a very suspicious character and you suggested you needed protection."

"But I never hired you."

"No law says I can't make sure you're safe."

"How come I haven't seen you tailing me?"

"Because I'm good." He suppressed a smile, thinking of Jennifer outside in the van.

Jamey brushed a wisp of hair out of her eyes and stared out the window. "I went to the pawn shop because I'm running low on money. It cost a lot to keep up a house and it needs some work. I sold some old jewelry I'd inherited from my grandmother."

When she wouldn't look at him, he took a deep breath. "Why do you insist on lying to me?" He stood and changed the subject. "Does Mark know about Carl?"

She shook her head. "No."

"Don't you think you should tell him?"

"Why should I have to tell Mark anything? He doesn't own me." She waved a hand in the air.

"You told me Carl was possessive. What if he catches Mark and you together?"

"Mark wouldn't be in danger. I would," she snorted, hooking a thumb toward her chest.

Hawkman shot her a disgusted glare. "Jamey, you haven't told me a word of truth since the day you entered my office. How can I believe that?" He headed toward the door. "Meanwhile, keep an eye on Carl's movements. Call me on the cell phone when he gets here, if he does."

He headed for the 4X4. Never had he encountered such a woman. She drove him nuts with her fabricated stories. He turned on the ignition and let out a long sigh, wondering why he even cared. "Because it's nagging the hell out of me, that's why," he muttered, slapping the steering wheel with the palms of his hands.

If Jamey pawned stolen diamonds at Kaufmann's and he turned greedy, they could both be in deep trouble.

Hawkman had run a check at the Oklahoma City Department of Vehicles and verified that the truck Jamey described did indeed belong to a Carl Hopkins. The first word of truth the girl had spoken. He'd pass the license plate number and information on to Williams, along with Jamey's description of the damaged rear end, in hopes that the detective would have his men keep an eye out for Carl's black Tacoma. They had no reason to pick up Carl, but it would be beneficial to know if and when he made his appearance in Medford.

Hawkman sensed from Jamey's description of the man that he was very egotistical. Obviously, though, he'd underestimated Jamey's mental capacity to use a computer. She took her lessons to heart and had tracked him, just like he'd taught her.

Jamey still hadn't convinced him of Mark's safety. What if Carl discovered them in bed at her place and flew into a jealous rage?

"Oh God, what a mess," he mumbled.

❦

Jamey came out the back door, wearing the long, lightweight cloak that she usually wore to cover her uniform. She'd just reached her car when Mark drove up. He got out of his Honda and started toward her.

Jamey pulled the cloak close to her body and pointed at his dirty clothes holding her nose. "I told you not to come over here with that filth. You stink like a cattle barn. Go home and shower," she stated, climbing into her car.

He stood scratching his head. "Why are you going to work so early?"

"Your dad called. He needs me tonight because one of the girls called in sick. I'll see you later after you've cleaned up. And don't you dare go into my house until you do."

She'd reluctantly given Mark a key to her place, but felt it a better alternative than her going to his tiny apartment. Her thoughts on Mark, she turned onto Main street when suddenly she caught her breath. "Oh my God, there he is!" she gasped.

Two cars ahead sat a black Tacoma waiting for the light to change.

CHAPTER SIXTEEN

When the black truck turned the corner, Jamey could see an older man in the driver's seat. She exhaled with relief when a second glance assured her that the tailgate of the vehicle was undamaged.

But, tomorrow for sure, Carl could be roaming the streets. Even tonight he might go bar hopping. What if he happened to stroll into Curly's? What would she do?

That would be the time she'd like to have Hawkman as her body guard. Jamey could just picture the horror on Carl's face if the one-eyed, mean appearing man grabbed his shirt and told him to get the hell out of there. She sighed, knowing she didn't have the luxury of Hawkman's protection. So, she'd just have to hide or escape out the back door if Carl came into the bar.

On the positive side, she had an unlisted phone number and hadn't filed the deed to the house yet. That could delay Carl's finding her address if he tried through public records.

Hawkman left Jamey's and headed for the pawn shop. He doubted he'd get much information out of Kaufmann, but he'd give it a whirl. As he cruised through the main part of town, he kept alert for a suspicious looking vehicle. He spotted the Zankers in their Tacoma, but none that matched the description of Carl's. He unsnapped his cell phone from his belt and hit a memory button.

"Jennifer, how's it going?"

"Hi," she said. "I'm parked out front at Curly's."

"Jamey's at work already? That's odd, she doesn't usually go in this early."

"Curly must have needed her."

"That's possible. I just arrived at the pawn shop, but I have a sneaking suspicion Kaufmann won't give me the time of day without Williams being present. Also, Jamey informed me that Hopkins is on his way north. But it's a long haul from Los Angeles and I don't expect him to roll into town until late tonight or early tomorrow. By any chance have you seen a black Tacoma with a skinned up tail gate parked nearby?"

A moment's silent elapsed. "No, I don't see anything of that description."

"I think it would be okay for you to head on home. I probably won't be long here. And, don't wait up for me tonight. I'll hang around until I'm sure Jamey is home safe and sound.

"Okay, I'll run by and pick up that list of groceries you forgot."

"Sorry about that. Had other things on my mind."

Jennifer laughed. "You're forgiven. See you tomorrow morning."

Hawkman clipped his phone back on his belt and left the truck. When he entered the shop, he noted the sound of the bell above his head. He waited a few moments to let his sight adjust to the dim lighting before stepping to the counter. Nothing had changed since the last time he'd visited this shop two years ago when Sam wanted a pair of very expensive binoculars. He'd found them here for about half the retail price.

Ludwig Kaufmann glanced up and smiled. "Hello, Mr. Casey. It's been a long time since you've been here." He held out his hand and the two men shook.

"Good seeing you, Mr. Kaufmann. How's business?"

He shrugged his thin shoulders. "Some days good, some bad. What brings you in today? If I remember correctly, you bought a pair of binoculars for your son the last time you visited me. And that's been awhile."

"You're right and they were a very good buy. Sam is still enjoying them." Hawkman shifted his weight and leaned forward, placing both his palms on the counter. "I'm not here to purchase anything today, but would like to ask some questions about one of your clients."

Kaufmann frowned and hesitated for a moment. "It's unusual to have someone other than the police ask questions about my customers. I realize you help the authorities out sometimes, but I don't have to answer anything I don't think appropriate without a law authority present."

Hawkman felt his stomach squeeze. If he'd still been in the Agency, he wouldn't have to put up with this type of response. "I realize that."

"Which client and what is it you need to know?"

"Did you purchase any jewelry or loose gems from a young woman named Jamey Schyler?"

Hawkman noticed a slight tic at the corner of Kaufmann's mouth before he spoke.

"Why do you need to know this information? Is there something wrong?"

"No. But maybe you can help me clear up some problems before something does go awry."

"I don't believe I should say anything more on the subject."

Hawkman feared this type of response and raised his hands off the counter. "I understand. Thanks." He left the store, but his inner sense told him something had definitely transpired between the pawn shop owner and Jamey Schyler.

He drove straight to Curly's, figuring he had no reason to switch vehicles as he wasn't hiding from Jamey tonight. Jennifer had left, so he circled through the alley and spotted Jamey's car, then drove around to the front and parked. He stayed in the truck for close to an hour, observing the coming and going of the customers, before he meandered onto the patio. The band would soon rip the air with its loud music, so he decided to take a far corner seat outside instead of rupturing his ear drums inside. Jamey scurried out to take orders and appeared surprised, yet pleased, to see him. Later, giving him a warm smile, she delivered his beer and hot wings.

The night passed without incident and Hawkman told Jamey he'd follow her home. Relieved to see Mark's car parked at the cottage, he waited for her to get inside and flip the porch light off and on before he took off for Copco Lake. He wondered how long it would take Mark to see through Jamey's lies. The young man seemed totally infatuated with her, making it harder for him to recognize her faults.

The next morning, shortly after Jennifer left, Hawkman crawled out of bed. He showered, went to the kitchen, had a cup of coffee, then wandered out on the deck to the aviary. Pretty Girl flapped her wings in anticipation. "I know, girl, you're ready to hunt, but I can't take you out today. Maybe tomorrow." He felt guilty for having neglected the falcon and promised himself he'd take her hunting in the next few days.

After supplying her with food and fresh water, he went into the kitchen and picked up the portable phone. He reached Detective Williams and told him about his visit to the pawn shop.

"So you have no idea what she hocked?"

"Nope. I have my suspicions. But to get any straight answers, I've got to have some sort of law authority with me."

"Yeah, that figures. I'll go over with you next week."

"Thanks."

After hanging up, Hawkman puttered around the kitchen, fixing scrambled eggs and toast. He rinsed out his plate and had just set it in the sink when the phone rang.

"Yeah, Hawkman speaking."

"Williams here. You better get into town. I've got faxes running out the kazoo and from what I've read so far, we need to pay Mr. Ludwig Kaufmann a visit today. Also, I know who ransacked Ms. Shyler's place."

"I'll be there within the hour." He dropped the phone, stuffed a handful of toothpicks into his shirt pocket, slapped on his hat and charged out the door.

Carl Hopkins felt like he couldn't drive another mile and checked into a small motel on the outskirts of Ashland, Oregon.

He'd heard about this picturesque town with its Shakespearean productions, but at the moment, he had other things on his mind, plus he needed some food and sleep. The long drive from Los Angeles had sapped him of his strength, and his shoulder ached like hell.

Before going to his room, he stopped at a fast food drive-in and took the meal back to his motel. The room didn't have a computer outlet, so he had to splice into the phone line before using his lap top. While it booted up, he munched on the hamburger and fries, thinking about Tina.

She'd made noises about coming with him, but he'd had enough trouble with one beautiful woman. He definitely didn't need another. So, he discouraged her by pointing out how she needed to take stock of her life now that she didn't have Nick's support and might have to move out of her lovely but costly apartment. Recognizing the reality of his remark, she agreed to stay home, but insisted he call her with information about her friend.

Carl had told Tina a little about the diamonds, but led her to believe that there were only a few and of little value. He found it easy to convince her that he'd chased Jamey across the country because he loved her. They had tried to figure out why Jamey had gone to Medford, but he nor Tina had a clue. They even tried calling Medford information to see if she had a phone number, but to no avail.

When the computer finished booting up, Carl clicked on the Oklahoma newspaper icons he'd left on the desktop, but found nothing new about the diamond heist. He'd even gone into the company's web site listed in the articles and found no mention of the stolen jewels. It seemed the whole mess had been swept under the rug. But Carl knew better than to think the diamond company would ignore a couple million dollars worth of lost gems. They knew they'd eventually show up. Carl hoped Jamey hadn't tried to sell one. That could really create a big problem. Too tired to start any new search, he shut down and went to bed.

The next morning, he didn't awaken until eight o'clock and

felt better than he had in days. The shoulder must be healing. It relieved his concern that he might have done some damage on the long drive. He gently removed the sling and took a long hot shower, letting the warm water flow over the injury. Refreshed, he dressed and replaced the sling.

He needed to find Jamey's address before he arrived. Again he turned to the National Newspapers on the computer and located Medford, Oregon. He pulled up the archives of "The Medford Mail Tribune" and put in Nick Albergetti's name. Immediately, the story of the shooting popped up. It stated an intruder had broken into the home of Ms. Jamey Schyler and tried to molest her. She shot him in self-defense. But no where did it give her street address.

After reading the article, Carl slapped his right hand on the table. "Damn," he cursed.

But the column seemed strange, so he read it again. They'd printed the 'home' of Jamey, not an apartment or condo. What did that mean? Had she bought a home? Good Lord, she might have sold off all the diamonds. The thought sent shivers down his spine.

With that possibility coursing through his brain, he quickly went into newly purchased real estate and put in both Schyler and Gray. But the search turned up a blank. He then went into the property tax rolls and still found nothing. Scratching his head, he wondered where to go next. Then he snapped his fingers. He'd hack into the police records. Of course, they'd have to give out the address when they were dispatched to the scene. He quickly jotted down the date of the shooting and went into the Medford Police Department. But to his dismay, they had him blocked. It would take him a while, possibly hours to figure out how to hack into the system. He didn't have time for that right now. He needed to get to Medford.

CHAPTER SEVENTEEN

Driving north on Interstate Five toward Medford, Hawkman spotted a black Toyota Tacoma up ahead. Curious, he pushed the accelerator as hard as he dared, closing the distance. Once he got about fifty feet from the black truck, he noted the scraped tail gate and dropped back. Yanking his cell phone from his belt, he hit the memory key for Williams and received a busy signal.

While pushing the redial button, Hawkman strained to see the occupant inside the cab of the black pick-up, but could only view the back of the man's head. The light colored hair fit Jamey's description of Carl Hopkins. Giving up on contacting Williams, he clipped the phone back on his belt and followed the Tacoma into Medford. When the black truck pulled into a motel, Hawkman drove past, made a U-turn and parked on the opposite side of the street. He watched the man climb out of the cab and stretch. He appeared to be about six feet tall and had his left arm in a sling. The fellow rolled his head, rubbed his neck with his free hand, then took off toward the motel office. His appearance pretty well clinched the identity for Hawkman. However, the guy looked more like a jock than a computer nerd. Goes to show you can't tell by looks.

Within a few minutes, Carl returned to his truck and drove to one of the units. Hawkman logged the sighting on his voice activated recorder, then waited approximately twenty minutes for Carl to come out of the room. When he didn't reappear, he became suspicious that the man might not know Jamey's address. If he planned on doing a search through the computer, he'd probably be surprised as Hawkman doubted Jamey had filed the deed to the house, she also had an unlisted phone number with no address. Both of these would eliminate her from the tax rolls or public records. Also, he knew several of the systems in town had been worked on to prevent hacking, but that didn't mean Hopkins couldn't find a way around them. It just might take him a little longer.

As he turned the key in the ignition, Hawkman spotted the office attendant come out the door with a bag of trash and head for the dumpster, which stood quite a distance from the main building. Taking a chance, he squealed across the road, bumped up the driveway and came to an abrupt halt in front of the office. He jumped out and darted inside. Quickly glancing around to assure the place was empty, he stole a glance at the registration book. Sure enough, Carl Hopkins had just signed in. Now he had a positive identification of the man and his truck. He and Williams would have to work fast. If they could get Kaufmann to cooperate, they might be able to get Jamey to spill the beans. He hurried back to his vehicle and headed for the police station.

A few minutes later, he sat in front of Detective Williams' desk poring over the reports on the ransacking of Jamey Schyler's house. Albergetti's fingerprints had been found in every room, even on the belt that had almost strangled the cat. "This certainly rules out a bunch of kids," Hawkman stated.

"Yep," Williams nodded. "And he obviously didn't find what he wanted or why would he have returned? I have my suspicions that Ms. Schyler didn't tell us everything."

Hawkman placed the report back on the desk. "I think you're right on some aspects. However, I don't believe she knew that Albergetti was Tina Randolph's lover."

Williams raised a brow. "She knows Randolph?"

"Best girlfriends since high school. Jamey stopped by and saw her before coming to Medford. When she quizzed Tina about her boyfriend, she said the girl avoided answering questions and never gave his name. Jamey figured the man must be married and didn't want his identity known."

"What a can of worms," Williams said, brushing a hand across the stubble on his chin.

"You got that right. And since Albergetti showed up, it appears word about the diamonds has leaked to the underground. Whether Jamey has them or not, her life could be in jeopardy." Hawkman decided to toss a bomb at the detective. "What would you think about putting her into protective custody?"

Williams jerked his head around. "We're talking tax dollars here."

"Yeah, I know. That's why I hesitated about bringing it up. But I just followed Carl Hopkins into Medford. He's holed up at the Village Inn. I doubt he knows Jamey's address, but I suspect he's trying to locate her through his computer. This man could be dangerous, and I'd like Jamey out of harm's way."

The detective sucked in his breath. "I'll have to think about that one."

"We can't sit on this too long. What do you say we go talk to Kaufmann?"

Williams rose from his seat. "You're right, we better get a move on it."

They took the detective's unmarked car and parked in front of the pawn shop. When they entered, Ludwig looked up from his usual spot behind the counter, smiling. But it faded when he recognized the two men. "Hello, Detective Williams and Mr. Casey, how can I help you?"

"We'd like to have a private talk, Mr. Kaufmann."

The owner limped to the front door, flipped the sign from open to closed and threw the lock. He proceeded to drag three chairs out from behind the counter and placed them in the middle of the floor, then waved his hand toward them. "Gentlemen, welcome to my private office."

Once seated, Kaufmann looked from one to the other. "Now, what's the problem?"

"We'd like to request your help." Williams said.

An expression of curiosity passed over Kaufmann's face. "And how's that?"

Hawkman leaned forward. "You have a customer, the one I asked you about the other day, Ms. Jasmine Louise Schyler. She's been to see you on at least two occasions."

Kaufmann frowned and leaned back in his chair. "Yes. I've done business with Ms. Schyler."

"What kind of business?" Williams asked.

"I've bought jewelry from her."

"Any loose diamonds?"

"As a matter of fact, yes I have. May I ask how you knew this?"

Williams narrowed his eyes. "We've done our homework."

Kaufmann immediately straightened in his seat. "I see. And what led to this query?"

"We have reason to believe the diamond Ms. Schyler sold you was stolen."

Kaufmann studied Williams' face. "I checked the marking against my list and found nothing."

"If your list is over two months old, the number wouldn't be there If you'll give me the identification mark on the stone, I can check it out. There were over two million dollars worth of diamonds stolen in Oklahoma City. We have reason to believe that Ms. Schyler has those gems."

Kaufmann took an audible breath. "Oh my. She sold me only one. However, I got the impression that she had another." He shook his head and mumbled. "But two million dollars worth? That's quite a haul."

Hawkman remained silent, listening to the conversation. Then he leaned forward and rested his arms on his knees. "Mr. Kaufmann, did Ms. Schyler indicate that she'd be back?"

He shook his head. "Unfortunately, I don't think she likes me. I reneged on my first offer, then had to eat crow. I ended up paying her more because I made a big mistake of under estimating her knowledge of the gems. Eventually I did get the diamond. But I sensed she needed more cash."

"Do you have that diamond here in the shop?"

"Yes, it's in my safe. Would you like to see it?"

Williams nodded.

Kaufman brought the gem over to the men atop a piece of black velvet. It glistened, even under the faint light of the shop. "Would you like my loupe to see the marking?"

"I'll take your word," Williams said. "Write it down for me. I'll check it out. Don't sell it before I talk to you."

"Don't worry. Legally, I can't sell my merchandise for thirty days after purchase. This is to give my customers time to change their minds and buy it back, if they so desire."

"I knew that." The detective said, rubbing his forehead. "I think I need a vacation."

Kaufman put the stone away and Williams walked over to the counter. "If Ms. Schyler comes back with another diamond, don't let her know she's under suspicion. I want you to purchase the gem, then let me know immediately. We'll get your money back."

Kaufmann handed him a piece of paper with the number of the diamond. "I can most definitely do that, Detective Williams."

Hawkman and Williams left the shop and headed back to the police station. They were almost there when Hawkman's cell phone vibrated. He quickly put it to his ear and heard Jamey's panicked voice.

"Hawkman, Carl's in Medford. According to the computer, he's checked into a motel here. I didn't know who else to call. What am I going to do? I know he's going to find me."

"Calm down, Jamey. I'll be right over. We have some important business to discuss."

CHAPTER EIGHTEEN

After speaking with Hawkman, Jamey stood for several moments with her fingers resting on the receiver. His commanding tone made her nervous. What important business? She walked into the bedroom wringing her hands and stared down at Mitzi in her wicker bed. "I don't have much time, girl. Carl is only minutes away, and Hawkman is getting awfully close to the truth."

She reached down and fluffed the cat's pillow. Mitzi jumped out of her basket and purring deep in her throat, rubbed her head against Jamey's leg. "I know, sweetheart, I messed up your bed, but I fixed it." She laughed, picked up the animal and cuddled it close to her chest. "I'm going to miss you terribly."

Strolling back into the living room, she glanced out the front window toward the creek. That's odd, she thought. That woman in the van is out there again today. Could she be part of Hawkman's surveillance crew? Just as she started to turn away, the van's movement caught her eye. She watched it pull away from the curb and drive out of view. Within seconds, Hawkman walked around the corner of the building. Jamey grinned to herself. Thought there might be a connection. She dropped Mitzi to the floor and braced herself for whatever 'business' the private investigator had in mind.

Letting Hawkman stand outside the back door for a minute after his initial knock, she took a deep breath, then opened the door a few inches and peeked out. "Oh, it's you." She unlocked the chain guard and motioned him inside. "Come on in. Can I get you something to drink."

"A glass of water would be fine. It's getting warm out."

Jamey closed the door. "Go on into the living room and make yourself comfortable." She soon joined him carrying two drinks which she set on the coffee table, then plopped herself down on the couch. "Okay, what do we do about Carl?"

Hawkman stood by the window, looking out. "We'll talk about that later. First of all, the police know who ransacked your house."

"I hope they caught those brats."

"Kids didn't do it."

Jamey glanced up at him stunned. "Then who did?"

"Albergetti. His fingerprints were all over the place."

"Why?" she asked wide eyed.

"Looking for diamonds."

She stiffened and gasped. "Diamonds?"

"Don't look so shocked. Detective Williams and I had a talk with Mr. Kaufmann."

Her face paled. His stare bore into her, making her extremely nervous. "And?"

"Where did you get those two diamonds?"

Hawkman had it figured to the wire, so she might as well tell him. "Carl gave them to me."

"When? I thought you told me Carl didn't give you anything. Don't lie to me again, Jamey. And believe me, Detective Williams is going to find out if those diamonds came from the Oklahoma City heist."

She caught her breath and turned her gaze away. "So, what are you telling me?"

"That you're in serious trouble. You took off with the stash and that's why Carl's hunting you down, isn't it?"

"Well, this might come as quite a shock to you and Carl, but I don't have them."

Hawkman glared at her from under the brim of his hat. "What do you mean?"

She sat with her back rigid. "When Carl came staggering back into that room with blood all over him, he handed me the diamonds and told me to beat it out of there. I was to meet him at Rusty's Bar in Amarillo in two weeks." Taking a deep breath, she rubbed her hands up and down her arms. "I went straight to the apartment from the hotel, then realized this might be my only chance to get away from him. I selected two of the diamonds out of the bags and hid the rest."

He raised a brow. "You hid them in your flat back in Oklahoma?"

She nodded.

"Why didn't you tell Carl?"

"Because, I didn't want him to know I'd left. I told you he's in love with me and very jealous.

"You could have left a note."

"I didn't think of that."

Hawkman set the empty glass on the coffee table and clenched his hands into fists. It took everything he had to keep from yanking this young woman off the couch and shaking her violently. Instead, he crossed the room and took a seat opposite her so he could look directly into her eyes. "I want you to tell Detective Williams your story, then inform him where you've hidden the rest. That will give the police grounds to pick up Carl. Then Detective Williams can contact the Oklahoma City police and they'll retrieve the diamonds."

Jamey stared at him. "Right now?"

"Yes. Right now."

She scrubbed a hand across her forehead. "Can't you give me some time to think about this?"

He hit his fists against his thighs. "Jamey, I can't believe I'm hearing you right. Carl is hot on your trail and I'm trying to help you, but you want to think about it? I don't understand."

She stood abruptly. "I don't want to talk about this anymore. I'll call you tomorrow after I've had time to figure out this whole situation." She stomped through the kitchen to the back door and held it open. "Goodbye, Hawkman."

He arose from the chair and as he started to go out, raised his hand. "Oh, another thing. You've committed a felony by selling stolen gems. And since you've crossed state borders, the feds will be called in on the case."

She slammed the door before he could step across the

threshold. Her face turned ashen. "That means I could go to jail."

He nodded. "Yes. You're in a heap of trouble."

Folding her arms across her waist, she stood and looked up at him, tears rimming her eyes. "How much time do I have before they get here?"

Hawkman shrugged. "I have no idea. And Williams is talking about a search warrant."

"How long does that take?"

"It all depends on the judge and how fast Williams can convince him it's important. You might have twenty-four hours. But I wouldn't advise you to do anything stupid."

"Will you protect me from Carl?"

"I'll hang around, but I'm only doing it because I want you safe."

She reached over and pulled open the door. "Thanks Hawkman. I'll call you tomorrow."

He threw up his hands and left.

ॐ

Once Hawkman's truck disappeared around the corner, Jamey went to her car and removed the diamond pouches from their hiding places. When she came back inside, she locked the door and latched the chain, not wanting to be surprised in case Mark came by early, even though she didn't expect him for another couple of hours. She dragged the suitcase from the closet and fished out the bag of cubic zirconias that she'd hidden in the zippered side pocket.

Next she grabbed a small dark blue towel from the linen closet, spread it out on the kitchen table, then set one of the living room lamps on the corner. Dumping the stolen diamonds into four small piles, she sat down and removed a cubic zirconia from its bag. She compared it to one of the real diamonds. To the naked eye, one could not tell the difference. Holding them up to the light side by side, she closely inspected the stones. She'd learned from her experiences in the jewelry store that every diamond had a flaw, but the zirconia was perfect. But, one would have to use a loupe to detect the fake from the real.

Deep in concentration, she'd forgotten to keep an eye out the window. When the door rattled against the chain, she almost jumped out of her skin.

Then Mark's voice pierced the air. "Hey, Jamey, unchain the door."

She quickly rolled up the towel with the diamonds inside, left them on the table and hurried to the door.

"Oh, sorry about that. Didn't expect you so early. I always put the chain on when I'm in the shower, just forgot to take it off when I'd finished."

"Got out of class early today and thought I'd drop by," he said, giving her a kiss. "I think it's a good idea for you to lock up when you're in the shower." His gaze wandered to the table and before Jamey could stop him, he'd reached down and unrolled the towel. A puzzled expression crossed his face and he threw her a suspicious look. "What the hell is this?"

CHAPTER NINETEEN

Jamey stood frozen to the spot, her eyes wide as she watched the diamonds spill out across the towel. Mark stared at the spectacle, then reached over and roughly grabbed her shoulder. "I asked you a question. And I think you damn well better give me an answer. I want the truth. None of your lies."

Blinking back the tears, she stammered. "I'm in a lot of trouble, Mark. I need your help."

"Did you steal these diamonds?"

She shook her head violently. "No, but they are stolen."

He looked at her blankly. "You're not making any sense."

Brushing the back of her hand across her forehead, she took a deep breath. "I need to start at the beginning."

Leading her into the living room, Mark sat her down on the couch, then he took a seat in the opposite chair. "I'm listening."

Jamey clenched her hands in her lap and told Mark the story involving Carl Hopkins from beginning to end, leaving out the part where she'd switched the zirconias in her bracelet to the real diamonds. "Hawkman and Detective Williams talked with Mr. Kaufmann at the pawn shop and found out I'd sold him two diamonds. I think Hawkman suspects that I have them all, but I told him I'd only taken two and hidden the rest in the apartment back in Oklahoma." She took a deep breath. "He also fears for your safety in case Carl finds us together."

Mark stared at her. "What do you think he'd do to me?"

Jamey shook her head. "I don't think he'd do anything."

He eyed her suspiciously. "What do you mean, you don't think so?

"He's looking for the diamonds."

"Yeah, and he knows you have them." Mark got up and paced. "Did Hawkman buy your story about hiding them back in Oklahoma?"

She shrugged. "I doubt it."

Mark put his thumbs in the rear pockets of his jeans. "He's shrewd. It would take a lot to fool that guy."

She glanced up at him and threw up her hands in desperation. "What am I going to do? I don't want to go to jail."

He pointed toward the kitchen. "Why are the diamonds out there on the table? What were you getting ready to do?"

"I had them separated into several different bags, but thought I better put them into the original ones if I turned them over to Hawkman," she lied.

He rubbed a hand over the back of his neck. "Give me a little time to think about this." Then he waved his hand toward the table. "Get them out of sight, they make me nervous."

He stepped over to the window and stared outside while Jamey hurriedly sorted the diamonds and zirconias by size, then slipped them back into the two original bags. She felt relieved after telling Mark most of the story, more than she'd ever related to Hawkman. Tucking the two bags into the zippered compartment of her suitcase, she shoved the luggage into the closet for the time being.

Mark stood at the window for several minutes contemplating the situation. Those diamonds would sure make life easier. He'd need to find a fence to handle that kind of stuff. Shaking his head, he ran a hand through his hair. Stop thinking about such nonsense. It's illegal and would ruin your life. Besides, the Feds might have men watching this place. Jamey really goofed up by selling two of the stones to a local pawn shop.

He glanced at the woman he loved as she came from the bedroom. It made his heart ache to think she could end up in jail or dead. How could he protect her without getting involved and ending up in prison himself?

She pulled a couple of cold beers out of the refrigerator, handed him one and sat down on the couch. "I've got the little gems all tucked away." Patting the cushion, she motioned for him to come sit by her. "Come here and relax."

"How can I with all that's going on?" he asked. "Aren't you scared the Feds could walk in here any minute and haul you off to jail?"

"Of course, I'm scared. But think about it. They haven't arrested me yet."

"That's true, but you told Hawkman you hid them in the apartment and he's obligated under the law to inform the authorities when told something illegal has occurred."

"They can search that apartment until hell freezes over and they aren't going to find any diamonds. So guess what? They'll figure Carl discovered them."

He pointed at her. "Or they'll figure you have them. Why else would Carl come looking for you? Then, they'll search this place and find the damn things."

"But all that takes time. Meanwhile, we'll hide them in a safe and secure spot away from here in case the detective gets a search warrant."

Mark almost spit out a mouth full of beer, but quickly swallowed. "Don't get any ideas about my place."

"Sweetheart, just think of what a great life we could have with those diamonds. I'm sure there's close to a million bucks worth." She scooted close to him and ran a hand up his chest, unbuttoning his shirt. Feeling his skin quiver at her touch, she continued removing his clothes as she rubbed her pelvis against him. His mouth found hers as his fingers fumbled with the buttons on her blouse. Massaging her full breast, he kissed her ear, then played his tongue down her neck and chest. He moved his lips gently around her firm nipple until she arched her back and moaned. Removing her jeans he gently pushed her down on the couch.

After they made love, Jamey held Mark close and suggested

they hide the diamonds in his car that night. Even though he protested, she finally convinced him that it would only be for a few days.

She threw on her robe, fished the two velvet bags from her luggage, then sat at the kitchen table and put the stones into the four small bags again while Mark reluctantly slipped on a pair of jeans. He then accompanied her and stood guard outside the vehicle. Jamey switched off the interior light as the full moon gave all the light she needed to place one bag under each of the ashtrays and the other two under each corner of the back seat. After popping the cushion back into place, she climbed out of the car and locked the doors.

Back in the apartment, she pulled a couple of beers from the refrigerator and handed him one. "If Hawkman ever asks you any questions about the diamonds or Carl Hopkins, act dumb. I've told him you know nothing about this whole affair."

He rubbed a hand over his head. "I'm game for that."

She took a sip of beer. "Another thing. If the police search my place tomorrow or the next day, you won't even be in town. You'll be at school. It's a perfect plan."

Mark scrubbed his eyes with his fists. "I can't believe this is happening." Glancing at the clock, he headed for the door. "I've got to get back to my apartment. It's late and I have some studying to do."

❧

Jennifer watched Hawkman pace the floor and noted his silence. "What's bothering you?"

He stopped short and glanced at her. "Jamey! She told me she hid the diamonds back at the apartment in Oklahoma City. I don't know whether to believe her or not. If I tell Williams he'll contact the Oklahoma City police. If they search the place and find nothing, I'll feel like a damn fool."

"Well, where do you think she's stashed them?"

"Somewhere in that house or nearby. A million dollars or more worth of diamonds can be hidden in tiny spots. Think about it. Those are loose stones in a small bag or two. She could have them in her bra for all I know."

Jennifer snickered. "Please, don't go searching."

He shot her a look. "This isn't funny."

"Sorry, it just tickles my funny bone. I could just see you trying to grab a peek."

"Cut it out."

She put up her hands in defense. "Okay, okay. I know it's a serious situation. But this little gal has a way of pushing your buttons. And after having her under surveillance, I can understand why. Would you like my suggestion?"

He exhaled and his shoulders drooped. "Yes."

"She's pawned off only two of the stolen diamonds. So, have Williams get a search warrant. If they don't find anything at her place, you can proceed with the Oklahoma City apartment."

"Williams is ahead of you there. He already has a search in mind."

CHAPTER TWENTY

His jaw taut, Hawkman stared across the desk at Detective Williams. "I'm wondering whether searching that apartment in Oklahoma City would be productive. I've a hunch the diamonds are right here under our noses."

Williams leaned back in his chair, his fingers forming a pyramid on his chest. "What about we search Ms. Schyler's place here, first?"

"Yeah, and Mark's apartment, even though I don't think he's involved."

"Are you sure about that?"

Hawkman shot him a look. "I'm not sure about anything where Ms. Jamey Schyler's concerned. And Mark's so crazy about her, he'd do anything she wanted."

Williams stood. "I've got the warrant to search Schyler's place. We might as well get it over with. If we don't find anything, then I'll work on one for Mark's apartment, but I might not be as successful. I had a bit of trouble convincing the judge about this one as we have no concrete evidence that links Ms. Schyler with a robbery. I had to do some stiff talking."

"Which means you still haven't heard anything on the diamond robbery?"

"Nope. I even talked with a jeweler. And he couldn't find any records on or about that Oklahoma heist. I guess the company is keeping everything under tight wraps. Probably still running that courier through the grinder. More than likely we'll hear something soon."

"Hope so. Don't know how long we have now that Hopkins is in the area."

Williams stood and tucked in the tail of his shirt. "I have my men keeping an eye on him when they're not busy. But so far, he's spent more of his time in the motel than out on the street."

"He's hacking. Trying to find Jamey. He knows she's here, just doesn't know where."

The detective moved swiftly toward the door as he pulled on his jacket. "I'll grab a couple of officers and meet you out front."

Hawkman hurried out of the station and jumped into his truck just as Williams rolled past him in his unmarked car. He pulled away from the curb and yanked his cell phone from his belt and called Jennifer. "I'm heading for Jamey's place with Williams. I want you out of there."

"Why? What's going down?" she asked in a stunned voice.

"I don't have time to explain. But get going right now."

A few minutes later, when Hawkman turned the corner toward Jamey's, he noted Jennifer's van had disappeared and breathed a sigh of relief. Sometimes she could get real stubborn about leaving if she thought any action was about to happen. Not that he expected any violence to erupt at this time, but he worried about her safety.

He parked and climbed out of the truck. Williams motioned for him to take the lead as they moved toward the back. The detective and his officers stood behind Hawkman as he banged on the door.

When Jamey unlocked the chain and peeked out, her hand went to her throat. "What are you and the police doing here?" she gasped, staring at Hawkman.

"Detective Williams has a warrant to search your place."

Her eyes spit fire. "So you don't believe me? Well, just come right in and do your damn looking. Then maybe you'll be satisfied that I told the truth." She swung open the door and glared at each officer as they passed. Once they were inside, she stomped into the living room and stood there tapping her foot.

Her stare bore into Williams like a knife blade.

Hawkman strolled over to her side. "Why don't we get out of here and waste an hour? They should be through by then."

Jamey stormed to the kitchen, snatched her purse off the table and headed out the back door, but Williams called her back and held out his hand. "Ms. Schyler, I'll need your car keys, please."

Her eyes narrowed. "You mean that warrant covers my car too?"

Williams nodded. "Sure does."

She reluctantly fished the keys from her purse and dropped them into his open palm.

Hawkman took her arm and guided her outside. "We'll see you later," he called over his shoulder.

Jamey climbed into the passenger seat of the 4X4, her mouth turned down in a hard frown as she slammed the door and gazed out the window.

"Sorry, Jamey. Feel lucky that Williams hasn't arrested you."

"On what charge? I didn't steal anything, Carl did."

"Makes no difference. You sold it," he said, pulling onto the street and heading for downtown.

"That's a dumb law." She glanced at him. "What if someone bought a stolen item at a garage sale and didn't know it?"

"If the law discovered it, it would be confiscated. And there would be lots of questions asked."

"What about the money that innocent people lost?"

"Gone."

Jamey shook her head and stared out the windshield. Suddenly, she grabbed Hawkman's arm. "Oh my God, there's Carl." She flopped down on the seat, covering her head with her hands.

Hawkman had already spotted the black pick-up with the scratched tail gate and had slowed, letting several cars get between him and the Tacoma. "Yes, I see him."

"He's going to kill me," she sobbed.

"Not if I can help it. Just stay down for a moment, I want to see where he's going."

He followed the Tacoma around the corner and down into the older part of town. Watching him park in front of

Kaufmann's pawn shop definitely piqued his curiosity. Going down to the end of the block, Hawkman made a U-turn, then parked on the opposite side of the street where he could view Carl's truck in his rear view mirror.

Jamey raised up when Hawkman turned off the engine, but he pushed her head back down. "I'll tell you when you can get up."

It eased Hawkman's mind to see Carl enter the small mom and pop restaurant squeezed between a dry cleaner and the pawn shop.

მ

Carl left the motel, frustrated that this little town had installed the latest hacker proof stuff into their systems. It would take him a few more hours to figure it out. He drove down the main street into the older part of town and concluded that this city would suit Jamey; big enough to hide in, but small enough not to get lost. She hated Oklahoma City, because she thought it so huge. The only thing that kept her there was the good paying job she'd landed. He chuckled aloud. "And me paying the bills."

Turning on one of the side streets, he spotted a small cafe. He hadn't eaten since breakfast and it was going on three o'clock, so he decided to stop. Who knows, someone might recognize Jamey if he showed her picture.

Ordering a ham and cheese on rye to go, he asked the Asian waitress a few questions, only to discover that she understood little English. He glanced around and decided there would be no need to ask any of the help.

After paying his check, he lingered a moment outside the pawn shop window gazing at the many items exhibited. He hoped he'd never get to the point where he had to hock his valued possessions in order to eat. If he found Jamey in time, he'd never have to worry about money again. He grimaced and rubbed his aching shoulder. He'd better get some rest before continuing his search.

He climbed into his truck and slowly drove back down the

main drag, checking each side of the street before he got to the Village Motel. He'd paid for three nights in advance. That should give him enough time to search the town.

❧

Hawkman watched the man in the arm sling munch on a sandwich as he peered into the window of the pawn shop. Carl soon turned away from looking at the displays and climbed into the Tacoma.

When Hawkman started his truck, Jamey again glanced up from her bent over position. "What's happening?"

"Nothing much, but stay down. I'll let you know when you can sit up. Looks like he got a bite to eat and is now leaving. We'll follow and see where he goes."

They tailed Carl for a few blocks down Main Street until he pulled into the Village Motel driveway. Hawkman made a U-turn and parked across the street from the motel. Once Carl disappeared into his room, he nudged Jamey.

"It's safe for you to look now."

Jamey raised up and brushed swirls of hair out of her eyes.

Hawkman pointed toward the units. "Carl's in that last room."

She studied the sign. "Village Motel," she read aloud. "Yep, that's what his bill says. He's here for three nights.

They sat in silence for close to thirty minutes before Hawkman finally spoke. "I think he must be resting."

Jamey's gaze hadn't left the motel. "I wouldn't bet on it. He's probably at the computer trying to find me." Gnawing her lower lip, she glanced at Hawkman. "What time is it?"

"Four thirty."

"You think the cops are through ravaging my house? I need to get ready for work."

He raised a brow. "You're going to risk going in?"

"I don't want to stay home alone. Maybe you could hang around Curly's for awhile."

He shrugged. "Yeah, I can do that if you want. In fact, maybe I should take you to work so that Carl won't spot your car."

"That's a great idea. Tonight you're going to show me that I should have hired you for protection."

Hawkman chuckled as he drove away. When they arrived back at the cottage, they found Williams waiting. He pointed at the handbag she carried.

"Ms. Schyler, may I see that?"

Jamey sighed and rolled her eyes. Taking the strap from her shoulder, she shook the contents out on the table, then handed him the empty purse. "I'll be glad when you're through. The next thing you'll want to do is frisk me."

Williams raised an eyebrow as he fingered through the items on the table. "Officer Mary Jones would be happy to comply."

Jamey stepped back, fear flashing across her face. "You wouldn't dare."

The detective suppressed a smile. "No, Ms. Schyler, we're not going to hand search you, so relax. But if I get a report back that states those two diamonds you sold are stolen, you've committed a crime."

She clenched her hands at her side and watched the detective examine her purse.

He finally dropped the bag on the table and headed for the door. "I'd advise you not to leave the area."

Hawkman stared at Jamey, noticing her indifference as she gathered up the items from the table and threw them back into her purse. She isn't the slightest bit worried, he thought, and he too started toward the door. "I'll be in my truck."

She nodded. "Okay, it'll only take me a few minutes to get ready."

Hawkman hurried to catch up with Williams. "So you came up with nothing?"

"Not a damn thing, Plus, I really had no grounds to search that girl's place. And it could cost me my job if she decides to press charges against the department. We haven't heard a word from the diamond company and nothing has come over the wire. If it weren't for you telling me about it, I wouldn't have known about that diamond heist back in Oklahoma. I'm just going on your word and those newspaper articles."

"I'd say you're ahead of the game. And with Hopkins in town it makes the story more probable."

Williams rubbed his chin. "I wonder if he's left that room."

"Yeah, Jamey and I spotted him. He went to get a bite to eat. He must be having some trouble hacking into the systems. The way I figure it, the only way he could find her address is to get into the police network and find the dispatches that went out about the break-in and Nick's getting shot. I'm not a hacker, but know a few tricks and tried, but nothing worked. So it may take him a day or two to track her down."

"Yeah, they put in a good program. What about Schyler's credit cards and bank?"

"She doesn't have an account and is paying cash for everything."

"That's odd. We didn't find any money hidden in the house and she only had about fifty bucks in her wallet. Where does she keep her extra dough?"

Hawkman adjusted the brim on his hat and grinned. "Beats me. Maybe you should have frisked her. Jennifer gave me strict orders that I couldn't."

Williams threw back his head and laughed then climbed into his car, then his expression turning somber. "If Carl is so good at hacking, what about the paperwork Curly had to fill out when he hired Jamey? That would have to be turned into the tax records."

Hawkman rubbed the back of his neck. "I'd have to check that out. Curly has a big turnover of hired help. He might not even bother registering each new employee. Probably depends on whether they've requested him not to file or how long they stay."

Williams furrowed his brow in false seriousness. "Now come on Hawkman, you know that would be against the law."

Raising his hands in mock defense, Hawkman backed off. "Hey, I never said a word."

"I think it best you question Curly," the detective said. "He might think I'm after him."

Hawkman grinned, gave a wave and strolled toward his truck.

❧

Jamey quickly examined the bedroom and could tell immediately that her luggage had been disturbed. She shuddered thinking what could have happened if she hadn't moved those diamonds. At this moment, she'd probably be standing in front of the mug shot camera. Her stomach quivered at the image.

As she dressed in her uniform, her thoughts went back to Carl's arrival. At least she didn't have to wonder about his whereabouts anymore. It would only be a matter of time before he found out where she worked. Curly's place was well known and all he'd have to do is ask a few questions. Her name would eventually surface.

She'd been thinking about this moment and formed a plan. Her nerves on edge, she jumped when she heard the door slam.

"Jamey, you still here?" Mark called.

"Yeah. I'll be right out," she said, coming out of the bathroom and picking up the long cloak off the bed. Draping it over her arm, she pulled her purse strap onto her shoulder and strolled into the kitchen. "I'm glad we hid the diamonds last night," she sighed, adjusting the neckline on her uniform.

Mark jerked his head around. "Why?"

"The police searched the house today."

His face paled and he flopped down in a chair. "You're kidding!"

"Not only that, Carl Hopkins is in town."

He jumped up and pointed at the floor. "Did Hopkins show up here?"

She waved her hand. "No, no. Relax. Hawkman and I drove around while the police went through the place. We spotted Carl's pick-up on Main. Looks like he's staying at the Village Motel. Just remember, you know nothing about any of this." She leaned over and gave him a quick kiss on the cheek. "I've got to get to work. Hawkman's waiting."

"I thought I recognized his truck outside." He grabbed

her arm. "Jamey, don't go in tonight, it could be dangerous. You know Dad will understand. You've never missed a day since you started. Call in sick."

She shook her head. "I can't do that to Curly. He'd have a hard time finding someone to fill my place on such a short notice." Patting him on the shoulder, she smiled. "Don't worry, I'll be fine. You do your studies."

He got up and walked her to the entry. "How can I concentrate if you're in danger? I'll be down later."

"Hawkman said he'll hang around. Do your homework and I'll see you later." She gave him a sensuous smile and closed the door.

CHAPTER TWENTY ONE

Curly watched Jamey as she puttered around the bar preparing drinks for the customers. She seemed unusually quiet and not her perky self. It worried him. Even though he figured Mark could do better, he still liked this girl and her stamina. She reminded him of his Emma, bless her soul, busy every minute until those last days. He shook his head, crossed the room and set a dirty glass on the counter. "Everything all right?"

She forced a grin. "Couldn't be better." With that, she balanced the tray on her hand, circled around him and headed for the tables.

Curly smiled as he watched her deliver the beverages with the ease of a pro. But just as she headed for the patio, Hawkman shot through the door like a cannon and whipped Jamey around by the shoulders, grabbing the tray before it crashed to the floor.

"Carl just drove up. Go to the back. Stay there until I come and get you."

The color drained from her face as she retrieved the tray and placed it on the counter. She then disappeared behind the swinging doors leading into the kitchen.

Curly scurried toward Hawkman with a frown. "What's going on?"

"I may have to get Jamey out of here." He pointed out the window. "The man who's after her just pulled up front in that black Tacoma."

Hawkman gave Curly a gentle push toward the bar. "Get everything back to normal and if he comes in asking questions about Jamey, play dumb."

"Is he dangerous?"

"Not sure, but I don't want to take any chances." Hawkman positioned himself on one of the stools. "Gimme a beer."

Curly hurried around to the other side of the counter, popped open an ale and slid it down the slick surface toward Hawkman.

Only a few seconds lapsed before a tall, sandy haired man with a sling on his arm entered the establishment. He headed straight for the bar and took the vacant bench next to Hawkman.

Eyeing Curly, he called, "Hey, you the owner?"

"Sure am. What can I get you?"

"Understand you have a girl working here named Jamey."

Before Curly could answer, Sue Mosely, one of the cocktail waitresses, tapped Carl on the shoulder. "Hi there, handsome. I'm Jamey. What can I do for you?"

Hawkman twisted around and glanced at Sue. She had Jamey's name tag pinned on her uniform. He suppressed a smile and turned back to his beer.

Curly raised his brows and quickly waited on another patron.

Carl's jaw fell as he looked at the young woman. "Oh, I'm sorry, I'm looking for Jamey Gr-uh Schyler."

Her mouth turned down in a pout as she played the role to the hilt. "You mean I won't do?"

Carl put a couple of bucks on her tray and smiled. "If I didn't have to find her, I'd hang around. By the way, do you know Jamey Schyler?"

She shook her head. "Sorry."

He waved at Curly. "Thanks pal, I'm outta here. I'll stop by again when I have more time."

When Hawkman heard the door shut, he strolled over to the window and watched the black Tacoma pull down the street. Once it disappeared, he made his way to the kitchen where he found Jamey sitting in the corner filing her fingernails. "That little trick took some fast thinking. What if he hadn't fallen for it?"

Her eyes twinkled with mischief. "I thought about that. There's a lot of Jamey's around, and we don't tell customers our last names. But they might tell Carl there's a Jamey working here and one at some other place. So, I gave Sue twenty bucks to be Jamey for the night. Which, hopefully, would send him running to the next night club."

Hawkman leaned against the door jamb and rubbed his chin. "I'd say it threw him off for now. But my gut tells me he'll be back. I don't think it's safe for you to remain at work."

"I need the money," she said, slipping the emery board into her apron pocket. "And aren't you going to be out front?"

"What if he comes through the back door?"

She sighed as she brushed past him. "Customers don't come in that way."

He grabbed her arm. "Wait. Let me check the area first."

Hawkman scouted the bar, dining room and front patio before letting her back into the main room. He hung around for several minutes before going outside. Jumping into his truck, he circled several blocks, keeping his eye peeled for the Tacoma. Satisfied that Carl hadn't hung around, he drove back to Curly's and waited for Jamey to get off work. He'd no more pushed back the seat and gotten his long legs stretched out into a comfortable position when Mark pulled up. The young man leaped out of his car, dashed toward Hawkman's 4X4 and yanked open the passenger side door.

His face pale, he shouted in a quaking voice. "We gotta get Jamey out of there. That Hopkins guy knows where she works."

Hawkman furrowed his brow.

❧

Mark realized the minute he'd opened his mouth and let Carl's name tumble out, he'd made a horrible blunder. Slamming shut Hawkman's truck door, he dashed for the bar. He forced a smile at the patrons on the patio, waved at some of his acquaintances, then quickly headed inside. Taking Jamey by the arm, he guided her back to the employee's lounge.

"What the hell are you doing?" she said, yanking away.

"I just came from the gas station up on Main Street and Jack told me a guy stopped by and asked about you. From the description he gave, it sounded like Carl."

"Mark, hold on a minute. Carl's already been here."

He sank down on the couch and stared up at her. "So what happened?"

She gave him a quick run down of the episode, then laughed when she told him about exchanging name tags. "That definitely threw him."

He looked puzzled. "How long ago did this happen?"

"Oh, probably an hour. Why?"

"Because, I came here straight from the station that Carl just left. He showed a picture of you to the guys."

Her smile immediately faded.

He raked a hand across his forehead. "And then I really blew it."

She looked puzzled. "Blew what?"

"I just spouted off to Hawkman about Hopkins."

Jamey clenched her hands into fist. "You fool," she hissed

Mark, not realizing Hawkman had followed him to the lounge, looked at Jamey in shock when the private investigator stepped into the room.

"Mark, Carl's back and I want you to get Jamey out of here. Bring your car around to the alley," he ordered. "I'll meet you at her place in thirty minutes. We need to talk."

Hawkman turned and headed back to the bar with Mark at his heels. When they stepped into the crowded room, Hawkman nodded toward the man sitting on the bar stool with his arm wrapped in a sling. "That's Hopkins," he whispered. "Go ahead and I'll detain him long enough for you to get Jamey home."

Mark hurried out the front door as Hawkman headed for the vacant seat next to Carl. When he plopped down, Carl gave him a quick glance, but then directed his attention back to the bartender. Curly had obviously clued his help because when Carl flashed the picture, the burly man just shook his head.

He let out a disgusted sigh, then turned to Hawkman. "You were here earlier. Are you a regular?"

Hawkman shrugged. "Depends on what you call a regular?"

"Someone who'd know the help. Obviously the workers don't."

"Yeah, I know 'em."

"Does this girl work here?" he asked, showing him Jamey's picture.

Hawkman took the photo and pretended to study it, then handed it back. "She's quite a beauty."

"Yeah, I know that. I want to know if she works here."

"Maybe, at one time. Curly's got the prettiest girls in town. But they come and go. Hard to tell."

Carl crammed the picture back into his pocket. "You're no damn help either. This whole bunch has given me nothing but vague answers. What the hell's going on anyway?"

"Maybe they don't like you asking questions. Who are you anyway? I've never seen you before."

"I'm just a friend trying to find her."

"If you're such good buddies, how come you don't have her phone number or address? Maybe she doesn't want to see you."

Carl's blue eyes narrowed. "You know you're a pain in the ass, just like the rest of these people."

Hawkman felt the hairs on his neck bristle as he tightened his grip on his beer bottle. "I think you better be careful the way you talk in here. These people are all friends."

Carl didn't heed Hawkman's caution and pointed to Sue, the cocktail waitress. "And that gal over there with the Jamey badge pinned to her blouse. I heard someone ask why she'd changed her name. They all laughed like it was some big joke. So what's the deal?"

Curly edged his way along the bar and Hawkman hooked a thumb toward him. "Well, there's the boss. Why don't you talk to him?"

"What's the problem over here?" Curly asked.

Carl twisted around on the stool and immediately pulled

the picture from his shirt pocket. "Okay, here's the Jamey I'm looking for. Does she work here or not?" Curly took the photo, held it at arm's length, and squinted. "She sure is a pretty little thing. Looks familiar, but I can't rightly say. I've had several girls by the name of Jamey work for me. Why you wanna know?"

Grabbing the picture, Carl gritted his teeth and jumped off the stool. "Shit, this place is full of screwballs." With that, he stormed out the front door.

A 'good riddance' yell echoed through the room.

A slight smile curled the edges of Hawkman's mouth when he glanced at Curly. He then left the restaurant and noticed Carl's Tacoma parked across the street. Hawkman ambled toward his truck.

Carl's headlights finally pierced the darkness and Hawkman watched him make several maneuvers to get out of the tight parallel parking spot. He also noted the high squeal every time Carl stopped. Better have those brakes checked, he thought, as the pick-up finally zoomed past him.

Keeping some distance between them, Hawkman followed the Tacoma until it turned into the Village Motel. Parking across the road, he watched until Carl disappeared into his room, then waited for several more minutes before feeling comfortable with the idea that Carl had called it a night. Hawkman decided to take the longer route to the cottage in case Carl had spotted him. He veered off onto a residential street, keeping his eyes on his rear view mirrors.

※

Mark drove cautiously to the back of Curly's where Jamey waited by the back door. When she jumped inside, she'd no more slammed the door than Mark gunned down the alley and screeched around the corner heading for her house.

"Dammit, Mark, slow down. Carl hasn't even left Curly's."

"Sorry," he said, lifting his foot off the accelerator.

She hit her clenched fists against her thighs. "You and your big mouth. Why in hell's name did you mention Carl to Hawkman?"

"Because it scared me to think he might already be at the bar. I figured Hopkins wouldn't mess with that big, one-eyed cowboy. You know how intimidating Hawkman looks with that patch over his eye."

Jamey sighed. "What exactly did you say to him?"

Mark repeated his comment.

"So you didn't mention the diamonds?"

"Oh, no!" he said, shaking his head violently. "Do you think I'm crazy?"

"No, of course not, I'm just nervous." Jamey chewed on her lower lip in thought, then pointed a finger at him when they arrived at her place. "Now when Hawkman gets here, let me do the talking."

He nodded. "That's fine with me."

They hurried inside and Mark locked the door, then paced, looking out the window every time he passed it. "What's taking him so long?"

"Sit down, Mark. You're driving me crazy. He's detaining Carl so we could get here safely. Then he's going to make sure he isn't followed. Private investigators have a fetish about that type of thing."

Mark flopped down in the chair and exhaled loudly. "Yeah, guess you're right."

When someone knocked, Jamey grabbed her purse, and pulled out the Beretta.

Mark stiffened and stared at the gun. "Where the hell did...?"

She put her finger to her lips and stood behind the entry. "Who's there?"

"Hawkman."

She dropped the pistol back inside her bag and opened the door. "It took you long enough."

"I wanted to make sure Carl didn't follow me."

Shooting a glance at Mark, she grinned. "See, I told you."

Before stepping inside, Hawkman asked, "Jamey, can I talk to you a minute outside?"

"Sure." She tossed her purse on the counter and brushed

past him. They walked out to Hawkman's truck and Jamey leaned against the fender.

He stood in front of her, his thumbs hooked in the back pockets of his jeans. "What does Mark know?"

She shrugged, making circles in the dust on the truck with her finger. "I told him that Carl was an old boyfriend who never gave up and that he frightened me."

"He doesn't know about the diamond heist?"

"Of course not," she said, glancing up. "He'd drop me like a hot potato if he knew about that."

Hawkman rocked back on the heels of his boots. "I tried to find you a place through the protection program, but Williams didn't go for it. Let's just hope Carl doesn't find you and try anything." Hawkman's gaze lifted to her face. "The police will be searching the Oklahoma apartment within the next two days. I need to tell the detective where you hid the diamonds."

She turned her back to him. "The living room drapes are hung on a fancy big rod with a decoration on each tip. Those little eagles pop off. I put a sack into each end."

He stared at the back of her head. "I hope to hell you're telling me the truth," he said. "Otherwise, you're going to be in a heap of big trouble."

She whirled around with her hands on her hips. "Why would I lie?"

"Let's not get into that, Jamey."

"You know," she said, picking at a fingernail. "There's the possibility that Carl found them. He knows I sometimes hid money in those rods."

"Then, why would he be out here looking for you?"

"You still don't believe that he's in love with me?"

"As a man, I don't buy it. If some gal hauled off and left me in the hospital without a word and I later found the loot at the apartment, I damn sure wouldn't go trying to find her. I'd get the hell out of there real quick."

She tossed her head and started toward the house. "Well, Carl isn't like everyone else."

Hawkman grabbed her arm. "I'm not through."

Jamey's eyes narrowed as she glared at him. "What?"

"I don't want you to go to work until Carl is out of the picture. He's no dummy and pretty well knows that everyone just led him on a merry goose chase tonight. He'll for sure keep the place under scrutiny now."

"So what am I supposed to tell Curly?"

He glanced at his watch. "I'll go talk to him if you promise you won't leave. And have Mark stay with you."

She folded her arms across her waist. "Well, okay."

"I think Curly will understand and it'll give him time to find someone to fill in for you until you can get back to work."

She dropped her arms to her side and shook her head. "Damn, Carl has caused me so much trouble."

Hawkman waited until she closed the door before he climbed into the 4X4. "She thinks Carl's giving her trouble. What the hell does she think she gives me?" he mumbled, slamming the truck door.

❧

Jamey locked up and leaned against the wall for a moment. Mark left his chair and came to her side, his expression somber.

"Well?"

She pushed some loose strands of hair out of her face. "He wanted to know what I'd told you about Carl Hopkins. I assured him you knew nothing about the diamonds."

"Did he believe you?"

"Of course."

"What are we going to do about those gems, Jamey? I'm a nervous wreck knowing they're in my car."

She held out her hand. "Give me your car keys."

He looked puzzled as he dug them out of his pocket. "Surely you're not going to bring them back into the house?"

"Shut up, Mark. Just give me the damn keys."

CHAPTER TWENTY TWO

Carl flopped down on the bed in his motel room, and automatically turned on the computer resting on the small lamp table beside him. He stared thoughtfully at the screen as the lap top booted up. The guy at the gas station had definitely identified Jamey from the picture as the new girl working at Curly's. It really pissed him off the way everyone had given him the run around. Did they think him some sort of an idiot?

What sort of story had Jamey made up? Surely she didn't tell anyone about the diamond heist. However, that woman could invent fiction. He also wondered if she'd found some guy to shack up with. A tinge of jealousy swept through him, but he shrugged it off.

He checked his watch and noted he still had time to check out some of the other night clubs in case the guy had made a mistake. But his gut told him that Jamey worked at Curly's. He shut down the computer, went into the bathroom and rinsed his face with cold water, then ran a comb through his hair.

As he stepped out the door, he noticed a familiar looking truck parked across the street. Where had he seen it? Then he remembered the 4X4 that had left Curly's the same time he did. Moving into the shadow of the large oak tree in front of his room, he studied the driver. Sure enough, he recognized the man with the eye-patch as the one he'd talked to at Curly's. Carl waited for several minutes, contemplating whether to leave or go back into the room. *What's he doing parked there anyway?* All the businesses on that side of the street were closed. Not wanting a confrontation with that mean looking guy, he'd about decided to go back into his room when he heard the engine of the truck turn over and the guy drove away. Keeping his eye on the street, Carl nervously hurried toward the Tacoma.

He stood with his hand on the door handle for several seconds and silently reprimanded himself for being so paranoid. That guy probably didn't have a thing to do with Jamey and could care less about him. And maybe the people at the bar normally avoided answering questions about their help. Especially, when some stranger, who might be a psychopath, inquired about the pretty cocktail waitresses. He sighed, rubbed his sore shoulder, then climbed into his truck.

He drove by a couple of the taverns, then went back to the one with the most cars in the parking lot. Once inside, he ordered a beer then strolled around checking out the help before taking a seat at the bar. Within five minutes, someone tapped him on the shoulder.

"Hey there, did you find Jamey?"

Carl glanced up to see the attendant he'd talked to at the station. "Oh, hello." He held out his hand. "I didn't get your name this afternoon."

"Jack. Yours?"

"Carl. No, I didn't have a chance to talk to her. She had the night off. I'll try and catch her tomorrow. Do you by any chance know where she lives? I'd sure like to see that gal before I continue my trip."

Jack scratched his head. "Well, you might ask Curly's son, Mark Spencer. He might know."

Carl raised a brow. "Is he her boyfriend?"

Jack shrugged. "Appears that way. Haven't talked to Mark for some time. Think he's going to school."

Carl rose from his seat and offered it to him. "I've got to get going." He motioned to the bartender. "Give this man a beer." He lightly cuffed Jack on the shoulder. "Thanks, man. Really appreciate it."

He paid the bill and left. A feeling of accomplishment surged through him as he jumped into his truck. He could hardly wait to get back to the computer.

Jamey went out to Mark's car, rescued the diamonds from their hiding places and tucked them into her purse. She then slipped under the steering wheel and started the car. Mark stood watching from the doorway, waving frantically as she drove away. "Where the hell are you going?" he yelled.

She took a quick look down the street to make sure Hawkman had left, then sped toward Main. Snatching Mark's ball cap he'd left on the car seat, she slapped it on her head, then rummaged in her purse until she felt the cold steel of the gun. She gripped the pistol for a moment, then her fingers continued fishing until she found her sunglasses. Even though it was dark outside, she removed them from the case and pushed the glasses onto her nose. Keeping her eyes on the road, she blindly searched for the extra set of keys to Carl's truck. In her haste to get out of Oklahoma, she'd forgotten to leave them at the apartment. She smiled to herself, thank God for the memory failure.

She glanced up in her rear view mirror as she approached the driveway to the Village Motel and her breath caught in her throat. Barreling up behind her was Carl's black Tacoma. Her stomach tied into knots as she hit the accelerator and drove past the motel while keeping an eye on the truck in her mirrors. When he turned into the resort entry, she breathed a sigh of relief. He hadn't even given her a second glance. Thank goodness she'd taken Mark's car and not her own.

After such a close call, she drove slowly, breathing deeply to regain her composure. Near the end of town, she made a U-turn and cruised back toward the motel, but this time, she drove into the lot. A dim light showed through the unit's window directly in front of Carl's truck. She grimaced, thinking that he probably had his nose in the computer trying to find Jamey Gray-Schyler.

Glancing at the Tacoma, she could see the blinking light through the rear window , which indicated the alarm was set. Even though she knew how to stop the noise from going off, her best bet would be to wait until he'd gone to bed. Why take the risk that he might come outside or need something from the truck. What's another few hours? She headed back to the house, but first decided she'd better have a good reason for taking Mark's car. She made a quick stop at an all night fast food place.

Back at the cottage, she found Mark pacing the floor, his face set in anger.

"Where the hell did you go? You know Hawkman warned you not to go out roaming alone."

She smiled and patted his cheek. "Honey, what's the matter with you? I'm not a prisoner and I figured we both needed some food."

He ran a hand through his mussed hair. "It just scared me when you left."

She raised her brows in an innocent fashion. "Why?"

"First of all I worry about you. And second, the diamonds are hidden in my car."

She waved off his concerns. "Don't worry. I took them out." Removing the hamburgers from the sack, she placed one on each side of the table. "Come on and eat before they get cold."

He stepped close and took her by the shoulders, staring into her face. "So, what are you going to do with the gems?"

She pulled away and sat down at the table. Concentrating on unwrapping her hamburger, she glanced up. "Don't know yet. But I have a few places in mind to hide them."

Mark kept bugging her until she finally screamed. "Mark would you shut-up. I don't want to talk about it right now. Just eat your food."

Even though he hushed, she knew he struggled with worry. And the best thing to do would be to take his mind off the diamonds. And she knew just how. After they ate, she began to strip. Mark watched with lust, a grin forming on his lips. Soon, she put her arms around him and coached him toward the bed. She knew he'd fall into a sound sleep once they'd made love.

❧

Carl studied the Medford telephone directory and found several Spencers, but no Curly or Mark.

"Damn," he muttered, slamming it shut. They must have unlisted phone numbers due to the business. He went to the computer and tried to hack into the unlisted file, but kept getting blocked. "What the hell," he mumbled. "Surely, this little burg can't be that advanced."

He rubbed the back of his neck and tried another approach. This time he got into the billing files, only to find several phone numbers listed under Curly Spencer, but nothing under Mark. Looks like this boy lives at home. So, I can rule him out as boarding Jamey. But he still might know where she lives. He jotted down the address and phone numbers of Curly Spencer.

Shutting down the computer, he went to bed and lay there wondering what this Mark Spencer looked like. He didn't like the idea of going to Curly's home in person to ask about Jamey, but having to go back over to that bar where they treated him like scum didn't appeal to him either. And he needed to find her fast

❧

An hour later, Jamey slipped out of bed, put on her jeans, her favorite shoes, a dark navy blue sweatshirt, tied a scarf around her head and snatched the already packed duffel bag from the closet. She quietly put her car keys and the note she'd written on the dresser, then closed her hand over Mark's keys so they wouldn't jingle. Throwing the strap of her purse over her shoulder, she tiptoed through the apartment into the living room. She unscrewed the hanging handles of the drape cords and removed the cash she'd hidden inside. Then she headed for the door. Suddenly, Mitzi let out a loud meow right near her feet. Jamey's heart almost leaped from her body.

"Hush, Mitzi," she whispered harshly. "You almost scared the life out of me."

The cat meowed again.

Jamey's vision, now adjusted to the darkness, saw the cat's

empty food container. She grabbed the box of dried tidbits and filled the bowl while giving the animal a quick back rub. "Sorry girl, I forgot to feed you. Tomorrow will be better." As soon as the cat started eating, Jamey sneaked out.

She trod lightly across the wooden porch and down the stairs, then climbed into Mark's car. He slept heavily after love making, so she didn't worry about him hearing the engine turn over. Hawkman or one of his agents wouldn't be around until daylight, so she felt pretty safe at 3AM, figuring no one would even know she'd left.

Arriving at the motel, she parked a couple of cars away from Carl's Tacoma and shut down the engine. She surveyed the area for any signs of life. Seeing none, she slipped the Beretta from her purse, checked the safety and shoved it into the front waist band of her jeans. After pulling on some surgical gloves, she removed the bags of diamonds from her purse along with Carl's truck keys. Flipping off the overhead light so it wouldn't turn on when she opened the door, she took a deep breath and stepped from the car. Crouching low so that anyone looking out the window of the motel room couldn't spot her, she made her way to the black pick-up.

Reaching the passenger side, she hesitated a moment. The alarm shouldn't go off since she had a key. However, she went over the steps in her head on how to stop it. Holding her breath, she unlocked the door. But to her horror, when she opened it, the cab light lit the whole interior. She quickly jumped in and slammed the door. The sound seemed to echo forever. Her hand flew to her gun as a streak of light flashed from the door of Carl's room. His silhouette filled the opening.

CHAPTER TWENTY THREE

Hawkman went back to Curly's and talked to him about the concerns he had over Carl Hopkins. Curly agreed the man sounded like a threat.

"You tell Jamey not to worry, she always has a job here."

"Thanks, I'll tell her." Hawkman said, as he left the establishment.

Driving away, an uneasy feeling swept over him. He headed straight to Jamey's cottage and circled the block. Both her and Mark's cars were there and the house was dark, which eased his mind somewhat. Hawkman then headed for the Village Motel where he spotted Carl's Tacoma in the complex. He parked across the street and observed the unit for thirty minutes. When he saw no action, Hawkman concluded Carl had called it a night, so he headed for home.

Driving the solitary road toward Copco Lake, he thought about Jamey's mess and it bothered him that he couldn't trust the girl. Jennifer had indoctrinated him with the new age of a woman's independence and strength, but Jamey didn't fit the pattern. She didn't trust anyone. Yet, she wanted his help. How could he give it when she wouldn't level with him?

Hawkman didn't sleep well and arose at the crack of dawn. He dressed, plopped on his hat and took a walk. The morning air was brisk and the view breath taking as the sun's first rays bounced off the quiet lake. He checked on the falcon then went back inside and sat at the kitchen bar with a mug of steaming coffee, pondering over Jamey's dilemma until Jennifer came into the kitchen.

She poured herself a cup and studied her husband. "You're up early and look worried. Did something happen last night?"

"I'm going to take over this morning. So you won't have to go in."

She frowned. "You didn't answer my question."

He glanced at her from under the brim of his hat. "Carl Hopkins showed up at Curly's last night looking for Jamey."

"And?"

He told her about the tactics they'd used to delay Carl. "It didn't set well with him and it will only be a matter of time before he finds her. I'm afraid it might be at a moment when I'm not around."

"Do you think he'll do her harm?"

He brought his fist down hard on the counter. "I don't know. I can't get a straight answer out of that woman. The people I talked to back in Oklahoma had nothing bad to say about either her or Carl. The landlord told me they were a quiet couple, paid their rent and never caused any problems." He stood up and paced, gesturing with his hands. "I'm up to my ears with Jamey's lies. I can't sort out the facts from the fibs. I don't think that girl has told me one ounce of truth since I met her. She frustrates the hell out of me." He shook his head. "Do you know how hard it is to work with someone like that?"

"I can definitely see why you're perplexed," Jennifer said. "Why are you worried though? You really don't have to do anything. She didn't hire you."

He dropped his arms to his sides, his shoulders slumping. "I know. But I'm involved now and my gut tells me something isn't right"

She pushed a loose strand of long hair behind her ear. "Have you thought about approaching Carl Hopkins?"

"That's crossed my mind. However, it would alert him that Jamey has talked about the heist. Then things could really go to hell. He could either run or go after her with a real vengeance. And the diamonds might never surface."

"Do you think she's got the gems?"

He nodded and exhaled. "Yes. But, she's hidden them well.

I've checked the banks and she doesn't have an account listed or a safe deposit box anywhere in Medford or Ashland. On top of that, Williams took a big chance searching her house and car. Especially, when nothing showed up."

She furrowed her brow. Why would that be a risk?"

"Because he only has my word that stolen diamonds are involved. There's been nothing reported to law officials by either the authorities or the diamond company."

"That's odd. Why wouldn't the company send out a bulletin?"

"I imagine they have their own investigators working and probably grilling the hell out of that courier. It also wouldn't surprise me if they had a tail on Carl Hopkins. However, I haven't spotted one."

"It sounds like the circle around Ms. Jamey Schyler is tightening."

He ran a hand across his chin. "I wish I could convince her of that."

❧

Carl rolled over and opened his eyes. He swore he heard a truck door slam. But that couldn't be his as he'd set the alarm. But to be on the safe side, he decided to check. Flipping on the bedside lamp, he got up and stood in the doorway for several moments looking toward his Tacoma. Seeing nothing suspicious, he decided it must have been a late check in. He closed the door and went back to bed.

That next morning, before getting dressed, Carl decided to call the phone numbers he'd jotted down from Curly's bill. One of them might be Mark's private line. The first two numbers rang the restaurant where a recording gave the hours of service. The next number's message sounded like Curly's voice. The fourth had the original message from the answering machine, a monotone voice requesting your name and phone number.

Carl slammed down the receiver and cursed. "Damn," he muttered. "They're screening their calls."

Frustrated that he hadn't come any closer to finding Jamey,

he leaned back in the chair and contemplated his next move. After the reaction he'd received from Curly's bar, he doubted she'd show up for work, so no sense in going back there. He needed a different approach.

Closing his eyes, he let his mind wander. The image of the guy with the eye-patch floated through his mind. He seemed everywhere. Who was he? Maybe Jack at the filling station could tell him. Shutting down the computer, he dressed and left the motel.

Since he'd filled his truck with gas yesterday, he pulled to the side of the station and parked. He peered into the garage area and spotted Jack with his head under the hood of an old Ford pick-up. "Hey, Jack, how's it going?"

The man looked up, a speck of black oil clinging to his nose. He wiped his hands on an oily cloth lying on the fender. "Hi, Carl. Brake problems with your Tacoma?"

Carl looked puzzled. "No, not that I know of."

"Well, from what I heard when you pulled up, I'd have those brakes checked."

Carl glanced back at his Tacoma. "Really? Sounds that bad, huh?"

"They're squealing like crazy and will be down to the metal before you know it. Then you'll really have problems. I'm surprised you haven't had a red light warning. You should have them replaced before continuing your trip."

"Okay, you've convinced me. How long will it take?"

"I'm not busy today, so I could have you out in an hour, hour and a half at the latest."

"Is there a place nearby that I could get a bite to eat? I'll just leave it here and go have breakfast."

Jack pointed down the street. "Yeah, just a half block down is a nice little cafe." He walked toward the office area of the station. "Let me get a work form. Oh, you said you didn't stop by for repairs, so, what'd you need?"

"Curious mostly. I saw an unusual looking guy hanging around last night. Had a patch over one eye, wears cowboy boots, leather hat and jacket. Looks mean. Just wondered if you knew him?"

Jack wrote out the order form and without even looking up, snickered, "Oh, yeah, everyone knows him. That's Hawkman. His real name's Tom Casey. He's a private investigator now." Jack scooted the clipboard over the counter toward Carl and pointed to the line. "Just sign right there and I'll get busy on your truck."

Carl stared at him. "What do you mean 'private investigator now'?"

"He used to be a spy with the Agency, but after the injury to his eye, he retired and moved to Copco Lake." He handed Carl the pen. "For sure, he's one guy you don't want to tangle with."

Carl signed his name and left the station in deep thought as he headed down the street toward the restaurant.

Mark rolled over and put his arm across an empty side of the bed. His eyes snapped open and he glanced toward the bathroom. The door stood ajar revealing an empty room. "Jamey?"

When he didn't get a response, he sat up on the edge of the bed and rubbed his eyes. "Jamey," he called again.

Still no response. He staggered into the kitchen, mumbling and put on a pot of coffee. "Where is that woman?"

He opened the blinds in the kitchen and looked down toward the parking lot. "Damn," he said aloud. "She's got my car and I need to get to class. Now where the hell did she go?"

Going back into the bedroom, he grabbed his clothes off the chair and headed for the bathroom. But before he got to the door, he spotted a piece of paper propped on the dresser with his name printed boldly across the front. He picked it up and flipped open the folded sheet.

His heart stopped as he flopped down on the foot of the bed, the note dangling from his fingers. He dropped his head into his hands. "Oh my God!"

CHAPTER TWENTY FOUR

Hawkman left Copco Lake, that uneasy feeling still hanging on from the night before. When he arrived in Medford, he went directly to Jamey's house, not taking the time to go by Stan's and exchange vehicles. Driving around the block, he saw Jamey's car, but Mark's was nowhere in sight. It seemed a bit early for the young man to leave for school, but maybe he had a test and wanted to review his notes beforehand.

Hawkman parked on the street where he had full view of the Toyota and the back door of the cottage. It wasn't long before Mark poked his head out and glanced around as if he were looking for Jamey's return. Puzzled, Hawkman waited a few minutes before he climbed out of the truck and headed toward the house.

He only knocked once before Mark, still in his undershorts, swung open the door. His expression turned to immediate disappointment. "Oh, it's you."

"Where's Jamey?" Hawkman asked.

Mark motioned him to come inside "She's gone."

"What the hell you mean, she's gone?"

Dropping into a chair at the kitchen table, Mark sunk his head into his hands. "She left her car keys and a note."

"Let me see it."

Reluctantly, Mark rose and handed him a piece of paper off the kitchen counter.

Hawkman unfolded the sheet, and scanned the message.

Dear Mark,

Thanks for all you've done, but it's time I get out of here.
Tell Curly that I really appreciated the job. It was fun working
for him.

I'm taking your car so I won't be recognized. Here are the
keys and the title to mine, which I've signed over to you. (Sell it
and get what you can.)

Please inform Hawkman that Carl has the diamonds.

Goodbye,
All my love,
Jamey

Hawkman pushed back his hat with his index finger and
glanced at the young man.

Mark frowned. "Do you think she's gone forever?"

"Sure sounds like it." Hawkman folded the note and held it
in his hand. "When did she leave?"

Mark shrugged into a pair of jeans and pulled a shirt
over his head. "I don't know, but it had to be sometime after
midnight. Once I'm asleep, I don't hear a thing."

Hawkman paced, his expression solemn. "Did she ever
mention a place she'd like to go?"

"We never talked about her leaving."

Stopping in the middle of the room, he stared at Mark.
"That note sounds like you knew about the diamonds."

The young man's head shot up, his face ashen.

"She's had them all along, hasn't she?" Hawkman asked.

Mark turned away. "I-I don't know," he stammered, walking
to the door and opening it. "I think you better go. But leave the
note. It's the last thing she wrote and I want to keep it."

Hawkman dropped the paper on the kitchen counter and
stepped toward the entry. "Even if you hear from Jamey, my
advise to you is not to leave town, other than for your classes."
Before he stepped outside, Mitzi rubbed against his leg. He
reached down and stroked her back, then closed the door.

Climbing into his 4X4, he figured there wouldn't be any need to hang around with Jamey gone, so he took off for the police station. Hawkman didn't find Detective Williams in his office, but noticed his rumpled jacket draped over the chair and figured he must be in the building. Helping himself to a cup of coffee, he sat down on the chair in front of the desk.

Soon, he heard the familiar agitated voice coming from down the hallway.

"Adams, take over the questioning. I've had it with that guy."

When the detective burst into his office, he stopped short when he saw Hawkman. "What the hell brings you in here at eight o'clock in the morning?"

"Bad news. Our little gal Jamey has done a runner."

Williams wiped a hand over his face. "Damn. She does have uncanny timing."

"Why?" Hawkman asked, raising a brow.

Williams picked up a paper off his desk and tossed it toward him. "This just came over the wire this morning. Looks like the diamond company has finally handed the investigation over to the authorities. It also has a list of the identification numbers and the two diamonds Ms. Schyler sold Kaufmann match up. So, I got on the horn as soon as I received this and requested a search of the Oklahoma City apartment. Haven't heard anything yet."

Hawkman shook his head. "Waste of time. I can tell you the diamonds aren't there."

Williams flopped down at his chair and exhaled loudly. "Then where the hell are they?"

"Not sure. Jamey left a note to Mark stating that Carl has them."

Hawkman related the morning's events. "I think Mark knows more than he's saying. However, I think he realizes he could be arrested as an accessory."

The detective jumped up and grabbed his jacket. "We need to talk to him. Let's get over there before he decides to skip town."

They hurried out to the detective's unmarked car. But when they arrived at Jamey's, the Toyota had disappeared.

"Head for his apartment, and if he's not there, we'll try Curly's house," Hawkman suggested.

They drove through the complex where Mark lived and saw no sign of the vehicle. Williams then headed for Curly's residence.

When they approached the house, Hawkman pointed at the car setting in the driveway. "He's here."

After several minutes of Williams pounding on the door, Curly finally appeared, his face solemn. "I don't think I want my boy answering any questions until I can get him a lawyer."

Williams held up his hand. "It's okay, Curly. The questions I need to ask won't require a lawyer present. We need to find out what he knows about Ms. Schyler."

"He doesn't know where she is."

"I'd like to hear that from him."

Mark sauntered up behind his father and placed a hand on his shoulder. "It's okay, Dad, let them in."

Curly hesitated a moment, exhaled loudly, then led the two men into a cozy living room, motioned toward the couch, and offered them coffee. Williams waved him off. "No thanks. We'll only keep you a few minutes."

Mark sat down in a chair facing them.

"Do you know where Jamey Schyler is?" Williams asked.

Mark shook his head. "No sir."

"Did you know about the diamonds?"

"Not until just a few days ago. I almost swallowed my tongue when I saw all those sparkling jewels." He ran a hand over his face. "It really shocked me and I insisted on an explanation from Jamey. She finally relented and told me about the diamond heist. I believed her and it scared me. I didn't want to be involved, but I didn't know what to do." He slapped his hands on his thighs and sighed. "Guess I just prayed it would all go away."

Williams studied Mark as he talked. "It doesn't happen that way. What did she do with the diamonds after you spotted them?"

Mark took a deep breath. "She hid them in my Honda, telling me they'd be safe there and no one would find them if they searched her place."

The detective nodded and glanced at Hawkman. "So that explains why we didn't find anything." He then turned back to Mark. "Did you help her hide the stones?"

He shook his head. "No, I just watched. But it made me very nervous to drive around with over a million dollars worth of gems stashed in my car. I told her last night she'd have to find a different place."

"And?"

"She didn't appear happy about the decision, but took my keys and went outside. I thought she'd come right back with the diamonds, but when I checked out the window, I spotted her driving off in my car."

"Is that the last time you saw her?" Williams asked.

He shook his head. "No, she returned shortly with hamburgers and fries. She told me not to worry about the jewels, she'd taken care of them."

"Did she have them with her?"

Mark's gazed at the floor, his hands clenched together. "I don't know, I didn't ask."

Williams leaned forward, his arms resting on his knees. "Okay, so you thought she was in for the night?"

"Yes sir. But when I got up this morning, she'd already left."

What time do you think she took off this time?"

"I wish I could tell you. We went to bed about midnight. I never heard her get up. All I know is what she said in the note."

"May I see it please?"

Mark removed it from his wallet and handed the paper to the detective. After Williams read the message, he put it in his pocket. "I want to keep this awhile."

"Can I have it back later?"

Williams nodded. "Did you give or loan her money recently? Help her purchase an airline ticket? Do you have any idea where she went?"

"No sir, to all three questions."

The detective took a deep breath and stood. "Mark, I don't know how much trouble you're in, but you should have reported all this to the authorities. I don't know if they'll come after you as an accessory or not, but you might want to find yourself a lawyer. Don't leave town and if you hear from Ms. Schyler, I want you to contact me immediately." He handed him a card. "I'd also like the stats on your car. I'm putting an APB out for it."

Curly looked like he'd aged ten years by the time he walked the men to the door. "And to think, I actually liked that girl," he muttered.

Hawkman patted him on the shoulder. "We all did, Curly."

When the detective and Hawkman were back on the road, Williams picked up the radio and put out an all points bulletin for Mark's stolen vehicle. Then he shot a look at Hawkman. "What did Jamey's note mean, 'tell Hawkman that Carl has the diamonds'. Is that a clue?"

"Yeah, I think so, but I'm not sure what it signifies. She knew Mark would eventually have to tell all he knew. However, it's hard for me to believe that she just handed the jewels over to Carl. She's gone to such great lengths to avoid the man and appeared to have a good reason to fear him. It's quite a puzzle. But my gut tells me you better pick up Carl Hopkins."

CHAPTER TWENTY FIVE

Carl, his thoughts on that tough looking one-eyed character, stared out the window of the restaurant and unconsciously forked food into his mouth. It explained why the guy seemed to be everywhere. Either Jamey had hired him or he was one hell of a nosy private investigator.

How much did he know? Any private eye worth his salt wouldn't hide a felon from the police. But so far, no black and whites had paid him any attention. Did Jamey tell him one of her far-fetched stories making him the villain? But where the hell had she gone? He hadn't even caught a glimpse of the woman.

He wiped his mouth with a napkin and motioned for his bill. Ambling back to the station, his gaze on the ground, he thought about Jamey. When he stepped onto the curb of the driveway leading to the gas station, he glanced up and felt the blood drain from his face. A patrol car sat in front of the big garage door blocking his Tacoma. The guy with the eye patch leaned against the fender chewing on a toothpick and staring at him. Another black and white had parked off to one side.

The big guy stepped forward. "Hello, Carl. I think Detective Williams would like a word with you." Hawkman pointed toward the man talking to Jack inside the garage.

Carl's legs felt like lead weights, his feet even heavier as he headed in that direction. When he got within a few feet of the detective, the man turned slowly and held up his badge. "You Carl Hopkins?"

"Yes," he said, glancing at Jack. He could hear the squawking of a police scanner coming from the gas station office.

Jack shrugged. "Sorry, Carl. I heard the APB out on your truck." He pointed toward the noise. "So, I called the police. I have a reputation to uphold. I can't afford to harbor some criminal's vehicle in my garage."

Carl's gaze darted from one man to the other. "I don't know what you're talking about. Would someone please inform me what's going on?"

Williams strolled toward Carl's Tacoma. The two police standing outside moved in closer, their hands resting on their holstered weapons. Carl's stomach jerked in spasms.

The detective rested his hand on the truck door handle and stared at Carl. "You know Ms. Jamey Schyler?"

"I-I know a Jamey Gray," he stammered.

"One and the same. Where is she?"

"I don't know. I can't find her."

"You sure?"

Hawkman stood at a distance, his feet apart and his arms folded across his chest. The man's presence made Carl's insides tremble. Even his shadow loomed across the floor like that of a giant.

Carl's gaze darted from Hawkman to the detective. "What do you mean?"

"She's missing."

He swallowed hard and almost choked. "But I haven't even seen her since I arrived. How would I know where she is?"

Williams threw open the door of the Tacoma and reached inside. He lifted out two velvet bags, which he held up for Carl's inspection.

Carl's mouth flew open. "Where...?" He stopped in mid-sentence and clamped his jaw tight.

"You know what these are, Mr. Hopkins?"

He shook his head. "No."

Williams gave him a sly grin. "Why Mr. Hopkins, you don't recognize the diamonds that you and Ms. Schyler stole back in Oklahoma?"

"I don't know what you're talking about? You're holding up two little bags. I don't know what's in them."

The detective carefully opened one and poured a few of the sparkling gems into his hand. "These refresh your memory, Mr. Hopkins? We found them hidden in your truck."

Carl's mouth went dry. This didn't make sense. Jamey would never have put them there after the robbery. She deserted him when she had the chance, taking the diamonds with her. When had she planted those in his truck? He felt like an animal caught in a trap. "Look, I don't know where those came from. Someone's trying to frame me."

Williams glared at Carl. "I find that rather odd, Mr. Hopkins. Ms. Schyler sold two of the stolen diamonds to a local pawn shop. We've traced them to the Oklahoma City robbery. It seems mighty peculiar that you show up, she disappears and we find the rest of the diamonds in your truck. Maybe you decided that you wanted the stash all for yourself and just got rid of Ms. Schyler." The detective returned the diamonds to the bag and held it up in front of Carl's face. "This here's a mighty nice little haul. Worth lots of bucks."

Carl stepped back, his stomach churning in fear. "Detective, I don't know what you're insinuating. But, I have no idea where she is."

❧

Williams noticed people gathering around and shouted to the officers. "Disperse the crowd and take him to the station." Then he turned to Jack. "Lock down this section of the garage until I can get a tow truck over here to move out that Tacoma."

"Yes, sir."

The detective went to his car and slid under the steering wheel. Hawkman climbed into the passenger side and waited until Williams radioed the order to have the vehicle towed to the police impound yard before speaking.

"You scared the hell out of Carl suggesting there might have been foul play concerning Jamey. Didn't you get the impression from Mark's note that she'd left on her own?"

"Yeah, but did she write it? I want her handwriting checked. Do you have anything we can compare it to?"

Hawkman scratched his side burn. "No. As a matter of fact, I don't recall ever seeing her handwriting. But I bet Curly has something. She'd have to sign her tabs at work."

Williams nodded. "Good idea." He patted his jacket pocket. "Also I need a jeweler to check these diamonds."

The detective drove to the Rogue Valley Mall, found a parking slot in front of Rhinehart Bros Jewels. The two men entered the establishment. The clerk's welcoming smile turned into a concerned frown. "Detective Williams. Is there a problem?"

"Would you tell Mr. Rhinehart I'm here."

"I'm sorry, sir. He's out of town for the day. Can I be of any assistance?"

Williams shook is head. "No, thank you. But, it's important I see him as soon as possible. When will he return?"

"He'll be here in the morning."

"What time?"

"Around nine o'clock."

"Is there some way you can leave him a message that Detective Williams will be here at 9:30AM? And, please, emphasize that it's very important."

"Yes, I'll leave a message on his answering machine. That way, he'll be sure to get it."

"Thank you."

On their way to the station, Williams glanced at Hawkman. "You're awfully quiet for a blabber mouth."

"Now you've got me worried about Jamey's safety. Do you think an investigation should get started?"

"She hasn't been gone long enough. We don't have a body so we can't be sure there's been any foul play. I'll drop by Curly's place as soon as he's open and see if I can get a sample of her handwriting, then I'll check with our expert, Charley, to make sure that she wrote the note. If she did. Our little gal probably did disappear on her own. Hopefully we'll get something on Mark's car soon. So what else is on your mind?"

Hawkman pushed back the seat and tilted his hat. "Seems odd she didn't keep those diamonds. My gut tells me she planted those gems in the Tacoma, then instructed Mark to pass the word to me. This way she's insured Carl won't be bothering her for quite a long time."

Keeping his eyes on the road, the detective nodded. "The criminal mind at work."

"I'll keep a sharp eye on Mark until we know for sure that Jamey wrote that note."

"Appreciate it. That will save me from having to use one of my men." The detective pulled alongside Hawkman's 4X4 parked in the police station visitor's lot. He turned off the ignition and rubbed the stubble on his chin. "If she's driving Mark's car, it should have been spotted by now. I better send a couple of guys out to the airport and have them search the parking lots."

"Good idea." Hawkman said, jumping out. Then he poked his head back inside. "You gonna grill Hopkins now?"

"Not until tomorrow. Think I'll let him stew awhile." He patted his jacket pocket. "And I want to get these diamonds verified before I really dig into him."

Hawkman gave a wave. "I'll meet you at Rhinehart's in the morning."

Williams nodded.

◦⋟◦

Hawkman opened up his truck door and let some of the heat escape before climbing inside. As he pulled onto the street, he wondered how much Mark really knew. Would he hold back to protect Jamey? Did he have something to do with her disappearance? All these questions nagged at him and he decided to head back toward Curly's house. Maybe Mark would open up without the police around. To his dismay, when he came in view of the residence, Jamey's Toyota was nowhere in sight. Under the strained circumstances, he doubted Mark would try to attend classes. So he headed toward the young man's apartment. Circling through the parking lot, he spotted the Toyota. He drove back to the street and parked.

He tapped lightly on the door and Mark opened it with a rush. "Jamey!" Then his face shadowed. "Oh, it's you, again."

"Sorry, Mark. May I come in?"

His shoulders slumped. "Yeah, I guess. Have you heard anything?"

"Nothing. Other than the police have Carl Hopkins in custody."

Mark's eyes brightened. "Has he seen or talked to her?"

"No. He swears he hasn't seen her since he arrived. No trace of your car either. It's like Jamey's vanished into thin air."

Mark ran his fingers through his already mussed hair and flopped down on the couch. "I can't believe all this."

"Are you sure she wrote that note?"

He glanced at Hawkman and furrowed his brow. "Oh, yeah. No doubt. She's written me several and I'd know her handwriting anywhere."

Hawkman's hopes rose. "Did you keep any of them?" Maybe he wouldn't have to wait for an analysis.

"There might be one around here. Let me check."

He got up and trudged into the small kitchen. Hawkman could hear him rustling through the cabinets. Mark soon came back into the living room and handed him a brown paper grocery sack.

"They don't say anything personal, just changes in work schedules or pick up something at the store."

Hawkman studied the handwriting. He didn't claim to be an expert, but knew enough that the note she'd left Mark definitely matched what he had in front of him. He tore the message from the bag and put it in his pocket, then glanced at Mark. "Did she ever mention to you what action she might take if Carl Hopkins came into town?"

"No. But I think he scared her."

Hawkman doubted that. But she did know Carl would stop at nothing, once he got on her trail. What puzzled him was her giving up the diamonds and then disappearing. Something didn't smell right. "How much cash do you think Jamey had on hand?"

Mark shook his head. "I have no clue. She didn't say much about her finances. But I do know she made good tips. And those can really add up over the weeks."

"Did she spend a lot?"

"Not that I know about. Certainly nothing outrageous."

"Would you know if any of her things were missing?"

"I checked her place and found that her good clothes, make-up and a little box that held her personal papers were all gone. I think she'd planned this for some time."

"Why do you say that?"

"Because I'm sure if she'd packed that night, I would have heard her stirring around. Even though I'm a heavy sleeper, that would have awakened me."

"That's interesting. I know you said she'd never mentioned any place she desired to go, but what if she'd inherited enough money to go anywhere she pleased. Did she ever say something along that line in just a casual conversation?"

Mark stood and hooked his thumbs in his back jeans pockets. "Never. She kept stuff like that to herself. I guess I really didn't know Jamey very well. She'd never let anyone break that hard shell that encased her. This whole mess has really bummed me out. And, the more I think about it, the more it bugs the hell out of me."

Hawkman studied Mark's face. "What did she tell you about the heist?"

He rubbed the back of his neck. "I better not say any more until I talk to a lawyer because it looks like I'm going to get implicated in this whole mess." He slammed his fist into his other hand. "Just because I saw those blasted gems and didn't report them to the police."

"That's understandable. But tell me one thing. Did Jamey tell you about being in the hotel room when Carl took the diamonds?"

Mark stared at him for a moment, then nodded. "Yeah. She was there and ran with them."

CHAPTER TWENTY SIX

Hawkman left the apartment figuring he'd pushed hard enough, and he didn't want to aggravate Mark or his dad anymore. The young man had been swept into a serious situation, but Hawkman felt Mark's life shouldn't be ruined because of two greedy people. True, he should have informed the police about the diamonds, but hindsight is always better than foresight. Hawkman made the decision, that if needed, he'd testify in Mark's behalf.

Strolling out to his truck, Jamey entered his mind. He'd learned enough about her at this point to know how deviously she thought. Before climbing into his vehicle, he removed his cell phone from his belt and called Detective Williams. "Any sightings at the airport of Mark's car?"

"Nope. Just heard from the officers. They didn't find it."

"You gonna be around for awhile?"

"What the hell do you think? I've got a mound of paperwork stacked in front of me that will take hours to get through. Unless, I'm called out on some very interesting case," he said, in a sly witty tone.

Hawkman chuckled. "I've got a hunch and if I'm right, I might need you in a while."

"Sure you don't need me now?"

He heard the plea in Williams' voice and smiled to himself. "Only if it pans out."

After hanging up, he jumped into the 4X4 and headed toward the airport. There were several acres of land before reaching the terminal that were sprinkled with warehouses and vacant lots. Jamey might have hidden the car on this property, knowing it might not be discovered for days. He took Biddle Road north off Interstate 62, and made a right on Knutson Ave. Driving slowly, he checked all the parked cars on the street and in the parking lots as he followed the roads around the industrial site. Finding nothing so far, he turned onto Gilman, the last street nearest the airport. He'd about given up, when suddenly, he spotted a car that resembled Mark's Honda Civic nestled close to a warehouse. He drove up the driveway toward the large building and the minute he could read the license plate, he dialed Williams.

"You can forget all that paperwork. I've found Mark's car."

"Do I need the coroner?"

Hawkman's stomach lurched as a thought he'd pushed to the back of his mind churned forward. "Hold on."

The phone still to his ear, he swallowed hard, stepped out of his truck and walked around Mark's car. "I don't see anything suspicous inside nor do I detect any odor," he said with relief. "But, it's locked up. I don't want to touch anything until you get here."

"Okay, where are you?"

"Off Biddle on Gilman Road. Behind the second warehouse."

"I know the area. Be there in half an hour."

Hawkman folded his arms across his chest and leaned up against the fender of his truck, chewing on a toothpick. He studied the large building and soon spotted a short burly man dressed in blue overalls walk out the big double doors and light a cigarette. He took off his hard hat and scratched a thick batch of gray hair. When he spotted Hawkman, he shoved the hat back on his head and hurried toward him, pointing at Mark's car. "Hey, that your car?"

Hawkman shook his head. "Nope."

The man mopped sweat from his face with a blue bandana and shook his head. "Well, whoever it belongs to better get it out of here by tomorrow. I'm gonna have it towed. I figured someone ran out of gas or had car trouble. Thought I'd let it stay here for a day or two so they'd have a chance to move it without a tow bill."

"That's mighty nice of you." Hawkman said. "How long has it been here?"

"Don't rightly know." He raised a brow. "I noticed it when I got to work at six this morning, cause we normally don't park on this side of the building. We load the freight trucks here." He pointed to a huge ramp that ran alongside the building. "We don't have a shipment today, so the car's safe for now. I've checked with all my men, and none of them claim it." He shrugged. "You a cop?"

"No, but I've notified them. They're on their way."

The man's eyes glistened. "You mean to say we've got an abandoned car in our lot that's wanted by the cops? Oh man, wait until I tell the guys about this!" He threw down the butt of his cigarette, crushed it with the heel of his work boot and hurried toward the big doors.

Hawkman grinned, watching the man disappear through the large entry. This must be the most excitement these guys have seen for awhile. Glancing toward the street, he recognized the detective's car turning onto the driveway, followed by a van, patrol car and tow truck. He spit out the toothpick and strolled toward the back of Mark's car as he waited for the vehicles to stop.

Within minutes and under the scrutiny of five warehouse employees standing off to the side, the technicians dusted for prints, then flipped open the trunk. Hawkman breathed a sigh of relief as he stared into the cavity which only contained some tools and a box of books. They examined around each of the door handles, then proceeded to unlock the doors and started on the interior of the car. When they backed out, one of the men told Williams that they'd found prints all over the car.

"Most of them probably belong to the owner. Once we check them out, I'll get the results to you." He handed Williams a set of keys. "Found these on the front seat under a napkin. I've already lifted the prints."

When the lab crew were through, they loaded up their gear and left. The detective waved for the tow truck to back up to the car. After giving the driver specific instructions, he walked back to Hawkman. "You look like you're concentrating mighty hard. What's on your mind?"

Hawkman pointed toward the airport. "I think our Ms. Jamey Schyler-Gray is long gone. She didn't park at the airport because she figured things would start popping as soon as Mark got that note. Leaving the car in a remote area would take longer to find and give her time to escape. I checked the airline schedules and a United flight to Los Angeles, left out of here at 6AM this morning."

Williams watched a jet fly overhead, the roar almost drowning out his voice. "So she figures she'll get lost in the big city?"

Hawkman threw up his hands "Who knows with that woman. Lots of connecting flights out of LAX. We'll have to search the records to find out if she took any of them." He headed for his truck and climbed aboard. "I'll see you in the morning at the jewelers."

ഛ

That night over dinner, Hawkman told Jennifer about talking with Mark and finding his car. "Tell me from a woman's point of view what you think Jamey has in mind."

Jennifer tilted her head in thought. "Hard to say. She was obviously a woman with a mission, and well planned, I might add. You seem pretty confident that she planted the diamonds in Carl's truck. In my opinion that's a bold move, not to mention risky. How'd she get into the vehicle without setting off the alarm?"

"Now that I think about it, when Williams searched her place, he had her dump the contents of her purse on the table. A set of keys tumbled out that looked like they belonged to a different vehicle other than hers. I didn't think much about it then, but I'd bet my bottom dollar they belonged to Carl's truck."

Jennifer frowned. "It still baffles me, from what you've told me about this case, that she'd leave without the diamonds. If her whole objective was to hang onto those gems, it doesn't make much sense."

"Yeah, something definitely smells fishy."

"Do you know if she has a passport?"

"No. But all she needs is a birth certificate to get into Mexico."

"Do you think she's acting alone?"

"I don't think so, but it's a real mystery who her co-conspirator might be. I've never seen anyone else around. The only people she's had any real contact with outside of me, have been Curly, Mark and Kaufmann."

Jennifer pointed a finger in the air. "Yes, but remember, she stayed home all day, only going out to run errands. Have you checked her phone bills?"

"Yeah. Nothing there."

Jennifer bit her lower lip. "She had a computer, didn't she?"

"Yeah, a lap top."

"She led you to believe that Carl was the great hacker. What about her? How much does she know about a computer? She could have been making all kinds of contacts online without leaving any record."

Hawkman rubbed his jaw. "You know you might have a point there. I better have Williams search her house. There's the possibility she didn't want to lug it with her and left it at the cottage."

"Here's another thought. What about Mark's computer? They were in and out of each others places all the time. She could very well have used his too."

Hawkman raised a brow. "This is getting very interesting isn't it?"

CHAPTER TWENTY SEVEN

The next morning, Hawkman awoke with a start. He sat up and rubbed his eyes, trying to remember what he'd just dreamed. But no amount of concentration made the image reappear to his conscious mind. He let out a disgusted grumble and Jennifer rolled toward him, putting a hand lightly on his arm.

"You okay?"

"Yeah, trying to remember what woke me up."

"Must have been a good one to make you growl."

"It had something to do with Jamey and that's enough to frustrate anyone. In the dream, she held up some item and laughed. But I can't picture it again in my mind."

Jennifer stretched and yawned. "Maybe it'll come back. Something will trigger it, if it's important."

"I hope so, otherwise it's going to drive me crazy."

She dropped her feet over the side of the bed and wiggled her toes in the fur rug. "I'll fix coffee while you're taking your shower. I'll be anxious to hear what you find out at the jewelers today."

As she walked in front of him in her short nightie, Hawkman eyed the curves of the beautiful woman he'd been so lucky to marry. He grabbed her arm when she reached over to get her robe from the foot of the bed. Pulling her down beside him, he held her close. Her long brown hair flowed across the pillow as her hazel eyes looked up at him lovingly. He kissed her and nuzzled her neck. "You're the most beautiful woman in the world and I love you more than you'll ever know."

Wrapping her arms around him, she pulled him toward her. "I love you too."

Later, her cheeks still rosy with love making, Jennifer shrugged into her robe, then poked her head into the bathroom. "Hurry, you're going to be late if you don't get a move on it. I'll fix you some breakfast."

With his hair still glistening from the dampness of his shower, Hawkman rubbed his hands together and smacked his lips as he strolled into the kitchen. "Man, that smells delicious. What a way to start the day. You and a big breakfast. We ought to do this every morning."

Grinning, Jennifer flipped the hot bread from the toaster onto his plate of eggs, bacon and hash browns. "We'd never get anything else done." She placed the plate in front of him, then stood back with her hands on her hips. "Well, did you think of the item in your dream?"

He raised his brows. "What dream?"

She laughed and shook her head as she wiped some crumbs from the counter top.

❧

Hawkman met Williams outside Rhinehart's Jewelry store at nine fifteen. The detective rattled the handle and knocked on the glass door.

"Here he comes," Hawkman said, spotting Mr. Rhinehart hurrying from the back of the store toward the front.

He let them in and gestured toward his office, then locked the front door. "I received a message from Ms. Jones that you wanted to meet with me this morning."

"Yes, I need your expertise on something," Williams said, heading for the office. The detective placed the two velvet bags on the big oak desk and took a seat. Hawkman pulled up a chair. The two men watched Rhinehart as he peered into the bags and let out a low whistle.

"Are these for real?"

"Yes, we think so. And I want you to check the numbers on them against this sheet." Williams said, pulling a folded paper from his inside coat pocket.

"So, there's been a robbery?" he asked, glancing at the sheet. "Odd, wonder why we haven't received our list."

"The heist was back in Oklahoma. We just received this information. I think the insurance and diamond company kept the raps on it in hopes of finding the culprits themselves."

Rhinehart spread a velvet cloth on the surface of his desk and dumped the bags of glittering jewels. With an instrument that looked like a small stick, he separated them by size, then made a quick eye count of the gems. He put the loupe to his eye and reached into his desk for a pair of jewelry type tweezers. He picked up one of the larger diamonds and took several minutes examining the stone in front of the loupe, then checked it against the list. He eyed Hawkman and Williams.

"Gentlemen. This one is on the list. It will take me a while to examine each one. Let me give you a receipt, that you have put these in my care for now. My schedule is light today, so I should be able to get through some of them. I'll give you a call as soon as I've completed the procedure."

Hawkman stared at the instruments that lay on Johnson's desk. The small jewelry pliers fascinated him and he couldn't pull his gaze away. He'd seen something like them before, but where?

Williams stood and held out his hand. "Thank you, Mr. Rhinehart. I'll be waiting for your call."

"Hold on just a second and let me get you a voucher." Rhinehart hurried into the main shop and pulled out a large receipt book from behind the counter. He wrote out the information, then handed it to Williams. "Hopefully, I'll be through by tomorrow afternoon. I'll give you a call."

The detective gave a nod. "That's good." He and Hawkman headed out the door.

"You sure were closed mouth in there," Williams said. "I noticed you couldn't take your eye off those jewelry instruments. What'd you find so interesting?"

"His tools. Something about them bugged me, but I've got a mental block."

Williams chuckled. "Welcome to middle age."

Hawkman grinned. "Yeah, it'll hit me when I'm driving down the street."

"By the way, I got a sample of Jamey's handwriting from Curly. It matched the note. Also, her fingerprints along with Mark's are all over his car. Of course, that really won't hold up in court as they were lovers." The detective let out a sigh. "I'm going to grill Carl this morning. You want to witness it?"

"Yeah, I'd like to be there."

The two men left in their separate vehicles and met at the police station lobby within a few minutes. Hawkman followed Williams down the hall to the interrogation area. The detective veered off into one of the rooms and Hawkman entered the next alcove. He closed the door and watched through the two way mirror as an officer brought in Carl and had him sit at the table opposite Williams. The detective glanced down at the open file in front of him, then raised his head and glared at Hopkins.

Carl hadn't been handcuffed, but he appeared tired and frazzled after his night in jail. His hair stood on end and he had dark circles under his eyes. His face pinched with anxiety as his gaze roamed the room and stopped at the two-way mirror.

Hawkman, out of human instinct, stepped to the side, even though he knew the man couldn't see him.

When Williams cleared his throat, Hopkins' attention riveted back to the detective.

"Looks like you're in a heap of trouble. Understand you had a confrontation with a Bob Evans back in Oklahoma City."

Carl looked puzzled. "I don't know who you're talking about."

"The diamond courier."

"Oh, him. I didn't recognize the name."

"He reported some diamonds were stolen and we just happened to find them in your truck yesterday. Do you have something to say about that? Or do you want a lawyer present."

"I didn't put them there. Someone's trying to frame me."

Williams leaned forward and stared into Carl's eyes. "Now who would just pick your vehicle out of the blue and hide stolen gems inside? Doesn't make much sense, does it?"

Carl squirmed in his seat. "I don't know how they got there."

"There were no signs the truck had been broken into. If what you say is true, looks like someone had a key. Who else would have a key to your vehicle but you?"

Carl's gaze couldn't hold William's stare any longer and drifted to the table top. "I don't want to answer any more questions without a lawyer present."

Williams closed the folder. "That's probably a wise decision. Do you have one in mind?"

He shook his head. "I don't know any lawyers in this state, plus I don't have any money to pay one."

"Very well, a lawyer will be appointed. More than likely he'll get in contact with you this afternoon. For sure no later than tomorrow morning."

The detective tucked the file under his arm and left the room. Hawkman joined him in the hallway.

"Certainly doesn't look good for Carl Hopkins," Hawkman said, as they moved down the passage way toward William's office.

"My next move will be to find Ms. Jamey Schyler. Those two were in cahoots from the beginning, I can smell it."

Hawkman rubbed his chin. "I think she framed him by hiding the diamonds in his truck. But why? There's something wrong with this picture. It doesn't make any sense. Important pieces of the puzzle are missing."

CHAPTER TWENTY EIGHT

Hawkman left the Yreka Police Station and headed for his office in Medford. Once there, he sat at his desk in deep concentration going over the personality profile he'd constructed in his mind of Jamey. It convinced him that she wouldn't give up those diamonds. So, why had she planted them in Carl's truck?

So deep in thought, he jumped with the phone rang. He quickly reached over and punched on the speaker phone. "Tom Casey, Private Investigator."

Williams voice boomed forth. "Hawkman, we got problems. Received a call from Rhinehart. Our little Ms. Jamey Schyler took off with a big portion of those diamonds after all."

Hawkman stiffened. "What do you mean?"

"Turns out that thirty of the gems in those bags were cubic zirconias. The remaining stones matched the list."

Hawkman slapped his hand down on the desk. "I knew something didn't fit. But it still baffles me that she gave up all but thirty. Suddenly, his dream flashed through his mind. Jamey stood in front of him, her head thrown back laughing as she waved a pair of jewelry pliers. The shimmering tennis bracelet dangling from her wrist. He hit the desktop with his fist. "Damn!"

"Something just meshed in your brain, I felt it over the phone line."

"You're right. I'd bet my bottom dollar that she's replaced the zirconias stones in her tennis bracelet with the real gems. I remember seeing a pair of those jewelry pliers fall out of her purse when you had her dump the contents on the table that night. I'm surprised you didn't notice them."

"Guess my mind was on diamonds, not tools of the trade."

"Jamey worked in a jewelry store back in Oklahoma City, so she learned some skills of the business. I still don't think we've got the whole picture yet. I suspect Carl Hopkins was only a pigeon in this operation. I'm heading for her house to see if she left a computer there."

"What good would that do?"

"If Jamey took a flight out of the area, where'd she get the money to buy the tickets? There's the possibility that the arrangements were made over the internet. I'd like to find out who she had contact with. We know the only suspicious call on her phone bill came from Oklahoma on a pay phone and that's no help. I also want to check Mark's computer. With her conniving mind, she could have used his to throw us off, if we got to close."

"Fine and dandy, but if she deleted the messages, we won't learn a thing."

"Then we'll find a computer guru. We know from history that deleted mail can be found on a computer."

"That's true."

Hawkman punched off the speaker phone, picked up the receiver and stood beside his desk, holding the phone tight against his ear as he drummed his fingers on the desktop. "Have you contacted the airlines?"

"Yeah, but haven't gotten anything from them yet. Expecting it any moment."

"I'll stop at Mark's place first and see if he'll let me check his computer without a subpoena."

"If he's hired a lawyer, I doubt you'll get to first base."

"Well, It might save his neck, so it's worth a try. Maybe he'll at least let me boot it up and have a look. I think he'd appreciate anything that might clear him.

"If he won't let you touch the damn thing, give me a call. I'll get a subpoena."

Then I'll stop by Jamey's and see if she left her laptop behind."

A moment of silence passed. "How are you going to get into Schyler's place?"

Hawkman smiled to himself as he lifted his pick tools out of the desk drawer and slipped them into his pocket. "Seems you've forgotten my background. A locked door is a petty obstacle."

"Sorry I asked." Williams chuckled. "This for sure will have an impact on the Hopkins' case."

"I won't even try to guess on that one. I'm outta here. Talk to you in a couple of hours."

By the time Hawkman reached Mark's apartment it was close to four o'clock. His heart dropped when he didn't spot the Toyota anywhere. But then he remembered Mark usually showed up about the time Jamey headed for work, so he parked and killed the engine. He'd no more pushed the seat back to give his legs room, when his cell phone vibrated against his waist. Yanking it off his belt, he spoke louder than he intended into the receiver.

"Yeah, Hawkman here."

"Good Lord, you don't have to break my ear drum," Williams proclaimed.

"Sorry about that. Mark isn't here. I'm waiting a few minutes, then heading over to the cottage."

"Well, hold on to your hat because what I'm about to tell you isn't going to make you any happier."

"Oh yeah. What's that?"

"Number one, there is no Jamey Schyler or Jamey Gray registered on any flights out of Medford or Los Angeles. Number two, her Beretta pistol was found in one of the outside trash cans at the Medford air terminal. Number three, my officers flashed her picture at all the employees on duty and not one of them recognized her."

Hawkman slumped back in his seat. "It's coming together."

"I'm sure as hell glad it is for you. Want to clue me in?"

"Have you got a copy of the passenger list for those flights?:

"Holding them in my sweaty paw."

"Good, I want to look those over. Got the subpoena ready?"

"Yep. Think you'll need it?"

"If Mark let's me look at the computer, we still might have to confiscate it if I can't get into some of the files." Hawkman straightened in his seat. "Okay, looks like Mark just turned the corner. I'll get back with you later."

He hung up and hooked the cell phone back on his belt. Mark pulled up beside the truck.and rolled down his window.

"Any word on Jamey?"

Hawkman adjusted his hat as he climbed out of the 4X4. "No. But I need to talk to you. Can we go up to the apartment?"

Mark appeared skeptical, but nodded. He drove into the complex and parked. Hawkman waited at the foot of the stairs while the young man grabbed his book pack from the back seat.

Once inside, Hawkman walked over to the computer. "Would you mind if I turned this on?"

Mark looked puzzled. "Why?"

"We have reason to believe that Jamey might have been corresponding with an outside party via e-mail. There's a possibility that she used your computer as well as her own."

Mark's gaze dropped to the floor and the fingers of his hands slid into his jeans back pockets. "I wondered about that myself and checked. There's nothing there."

"Would you mind if I looked?"

He shook his head. "No. Go ahead."

After booting up the computer, Hawkman sat down and began clicking through several files where e-mails could be stashed without the receiver knowing. He opened a strange looking file in one of the preference folders and found an e-mail addressed to 'AM' and signed by 'AD'. The message stated: "Sorry, I can't help you right now. Things are tight." The dated message indicated it had been sent and received during Jamey's stay in the area. Hawkman called Mark over. "Is this familiar to you?"

Mark read the e-mail, then shook his head. "No. I've never seen it before."

"Would you mind if I printed this out?"

"Go ahead. You think it has something to do with Jamey?"

Hawkman shrugged. "Hard to say. Anyone else had access to your computer these past few weeks?"

"Not to my knowledge," Mark said, watching the monitor.

Hawkman searched more and found another strange e-mail in a different folder dated a few days later, but still used the same initials. It stated 'Refer to previous post. Follow original plan. Send no more'.

Hawkman hit the print button again.

"What do you think these mean?" Mark asked.

"If they were sent to Jamey, it definitely indicates an outside party is involved with her disappearance."

Mark glanced at him with fear in his eyes. "Do you think she's in danger?"

"I wish I had an answer for you," Hawkman said, folding the sheets and sticking them into his pocket. "Don't delete those messages. There may be more that I can't find. It will take an expert to examine the machine innards and he might be able to trace their origin." He glanced at Mark. "Will it inconvenience you if we take the computer into headquarters? This information could well get you off the hook."

Mark rubbed a hand over his face. "Let me get the okay from my lawyer and I'll give you a call. If I need a computer for my studies, I can head over to Dad's place."

Hawkman nodded and shut down the machine. "Sounds fair. Give me a call after you've talked to him." He handed Mark a card after writing a number on the back. "You can always reach me on my cell phone." He turned toward the door, then faced Mark one more time. "By the way. What ever happened to Jamey's cell phone?"

Mark crossed over to his back pack and pulled it out. "She gave it to me. Said she hated it because she always misplaced it."

"Do you have the latest bill?"

"Yeah, as a matter of fact, I just got it yesterday."

"May I see it?"

"Not much there, because I seldom use it and neither did Jamey." A forced smile twitched Mark's lips as he picked up the lone envelope on the kitchen cabinet and handed it to Hawkman. "This is one bill Dad said he wouldn't pay."

Hawkman glanced through the print out. The bill covered the time Jamey had been there and nothing appeared worth noting. He handed it back to Mark. "You're right. It hasn't seen much use and there's nothing listed of interest."

"That's why she gave it to me."

"Thanks Mark, for your cooperation. Let's hope we find her alive and get this thing settled soon."

Mark frowned. "Do you think something could have happened to her?"

Hawkman patted him on the shoulder. "Well, at least we haven't found a corpse, which gives us hope."

The young man's face turned pale.

CHAPTER TWENTY NINE

A grin tugged at the corners of Jamey's mouth as she pulled out of the motel parking lot. She wished she could see Carl's face when the police discovered the diamonds.

Instead of turning back toward Mark's apartment, she headed in the opposite direction. Having surveyed the area sometime ago, she knew exactly where she'd park the car so it wouldn't be spotted for several hours or possibly days. Once Mark found the note and notified Hawkman, all hell would break loose. They would find the diamonds in Carl's truck and arrest him. But once a jeweler examined the stones and discover thirty of those diamonds are cubic zirconias, an all points bulletin would be put out on her.

Due to the energy crisis, the warehouse grounds had only a few faint lights glowing around the perimeter of the large lot. She cut the car beams as she pulled alongside the big building.

Airport security had tightened since the terrorist attack, so she'd wrapped her gun in a brown paper sack and would get rid of it before entering the terminal. Before getting out of the car, she changed into the set of clothes she'd brought, then took the dark brown, short-haired wig out of the bundle, gave it a quick shake and pulled it over her head. She noticed her hands trembling as she pushed stray hairs underneath the cap. Briefcase, purse and shoes in hand, she climbed out of the car. After checking the interior for any forgotten item, she tossed the keys on the seat, covering them with a napkin left from a fast food place. Satisfied she had everything, she locked, slammed the door and started walking.

Reaching the outskirts of the terminal, she checked her

watch. She still had a good hour and a half before her plane left, but with the new security rules, it pushed her for time. Hopefully, since this was such an early flight, it wouldn't be crowded. Spotting a trash can as she approached the entrance, she shoved the paper sack containing the gun deep into its bowels, dusted off her hands, then hurried inside. She headed straight for the first ladies' room she spotted. Pleasantly surprised, she found herself alone.

In front of the mirror, she tucked the tailored white silk blouse into her skirt waistband, then adjusted the collar of the navy blue suit jacket. Noticing blond hairs that had strayed around the rim of the wig, she pushed them underneath. Unzipping her purse, she fished out a small velvet bag and removed a gold necklace with a ruby pendant. Holding it up to catch the light, she smiled, then quickly fastened it around her neck. She stood back and scrutinized her new look. It pleased her to have that appearance of a professional business woman with a purpose in mind.

After slipping on the high heeled shoes, she flipped open the briefcase with the initials A.M. embossed in gold on the corner. She first made sure everything had remained where she'd put it earlier: the extra set of clothes neatly folded within a plastic bag, along with a small pouch that contained her make-up. The stack of business cards identifying her as Amelia Mallory, a Jewelry Consultant, were still snug in the compartment made for them, along with a yellow legal pad and a couple of executive looking pens. The large diamond, emerald and sapphire were secured inside small jewelry boxes, strapped to the inside by leather bands. She wondered how long she had before the report of the stolen gems would hit the news stands. Trying not to think about it, she folded a paper towel around the shoes she'd worn to the airport and placed them beside her clothes.

Adjusting her purse strap over her shoulder, she picked up the valise and started toward the exit when two women entered the restroom. Her heart skipped a beat when they both stopped in their tracks and stared at her. She prayed her appearance didn't reveal anything more than a hassled business executive running late. Or, had the word already gotten out? She gave them a forced smile, then pushed through the door and headed for the boarding gate.

Several people were in line at the x-ray machine, which made her breathe a little easier, even though she could feel the sweat forming on her upper lip. She dabbed at it with a tissue as she watched with interest when a couple before her were instructed to remove their shoes. The attendant then thoroughly examined the heels and soles.

When her turn came, she placed her briefcase and purse on the moving platform then stepped through the scanner. Holding her breath, she watched the attendant flip open her briefcase and glance through it. She forced a smile when he nodded and handed it to her.

Turning away, she let out a sigh of relief and hurried toward the walkway to the plane, thanking her lucky stars that she hadn't followed through with her original plan of storing the gems in a hollowed out shoe heel. The story about the terrorist who'd tried that stunt with explosives and gotten caught changed her mind.

꩜

When Hawkman arrived at the police station, he showed Williams the e-mails he'd found on Mark's computer.

The detective scratched his side burn as he scanned the messages. "Looks like she definitely had an accomplice."

"Yeah, but who? Mark and I ran a check through all his computer logs and couldn't find anything else referring to the initials A.D. or A.M"

Williams poked the paper with his finger. "Of course, you realize these messages won't hold up in court. We're suspicious of what they mean, but no jury will buy it."

Hawkman draped an arm across the edge of the desk. "They definitely don't give us any clues. However, don't you get the sense that whoever sent them is sending a message that he or she is being watched?"

"It appears as such. Got any ideas?"

"Well, I've ruled out that the messages came from Carl."

Williams leaned back in his chair. "I agree. She's running from him. Do you think Mark's involved?"

Hawkman waved off the suggestion. "Hell no, he's young and naive. His downfall was having the hots for Jamey. He got himself entwined in this mess after he met her. His fear is very evident."

The detective came forward in his chair. "So what's your conclusion?"

Pushing up the brim of his hat with his finger, Hawkman looked into his face. "I think there's someone back in Oklahoma. Maybe even connected with the jewelry shop where Jamey worked. This heist has been planned for a long time. They needed a third party and that's where Carl Hopkins fit into the picture. They probably figured the wound would stop him in his tracks and he'd want nothing more to do with Jamey. Especially after she just up and disappeared."

"Why didn't they just kill him?"

"I don't think they wanted to deal with a murder rap if the plan went sour. They just wanted him injured bad enough to buy some time, hoping Jamey could get across country and disappear before Carl got out of the hospital. However, instead of Carl turning tail and running the opposite direction, he took this heist seriously and wanted his share of those diamonds. So, with his computer knowledge, he traced her. Something I don't think they expected."

"How in the hell did she end up in Medford?"

"The way I figure it, her accomplice didn't want to draw attention to himself by leaving too soon after the heist. Jamey needed to cool it for a month or more. Her aunt's death came at an ideal time." Hawkman threw up his hands. "Perfect. Her own little hideaway for as long as she needed it." He raised a finger in the air. "However, things never go as planned and they've ran into some pot holes."

"You say they didn't want murder in this scenario, so how do you explain her gun?"

"Oh, I think she'd have used it if Carl had actually

confronted her, just like she did on Nick. Somehow Albergetti found out about the diamonds and wanted in on the take. She'd have killed Hopkins just as swiftly, then screamed self-defense."

"You think she's still in the country?"

"I doubt it. She probably donned a wig, dressed in a business suit and flew out of here under a fictitious name."

"She better have proof with the stringent regulations of the airlines now."

"I'm sure that was taken care of long before the heist ever took place."

"You think the initials on those e-mail messages mean anything?"

"Not sure. That's why I want to go over those passenger lists you got from the airlines. Are they handy?"

Williams shuffled through the papers on his desk for several moments, then finally tossed a bunch of stapled papers in front of Hawkman.

He picked up the sheets and thumbed through them. "This will probably be a waste of time, but I'll take a look and see if anything strikes me."

"Take them with you. I made an extra copy. Figured you might want one."

"Thanks." Hawkman rolled it up in his hand and stood. "So what direction will you take with Carl Hopkins now?"

He shrugged. "That will be up to his lawyer. Since some of the diamonds were returned, and it looks like Ms. Schyler took off with the rest, he'll probably get off scott free." The detective stepped out from behind his desk and tucked in his shirt. "That reminds me, Mr. Rhinehart has called several times, leaving an urgent message for me to call. Thought I'd just drop by his shop instead. Want to come?"

"Sure."

Williams took his jacket off the back of the chair and shrugged into it as he started toward the door. "So how did you get drawn into this mess?"

Hawkman followed him into the hallway. "I think she used

me as a front to defer suspicion. And that feisty little broad stayed one step ahead of me with her pack of lies. But it's pretty much out of my hands now. About the only thing I can do is help Mark. I'm sure neither he nor any of us will ever hear from Jamey Schyler-Gray again."

The detective let out a long sigh. "Now that she's disappeared without a trace, the police file will have to remain open indefinitely, in case we come up with a corpse somewhere down the line."

"Yep," Hawkman said, as they headed for the unmarked car.

When they reached the shop, Rhinehart hurriedly escorted the two men into his private office and motioned for them to have a seat. His expression somber, he sat down behind his desk. "I've just been informed by the Jewelry Association that there are more than just diamonds involved."

Williams looked at him puzzled. "What do you mean?"

Rhinehart fiddled with a pen on his desk. "The courier had some precious gems that he was carrying for another company. They're also missing."

The detective scratched his head. "You've lost me, Rhinehart. What are you talking about?"

His cheeks flushed, the jeweler continued. "The courier had a special packet containing a large rare ruby, an emerald, two sapphires and a twelve caret diamond. The dollar amount hits close to six million. The other company assumed if the diamonds were found, those gems would be among them. Unfortunately, that isn't the case, unless you gentlemen didn't show me everything you found."

Williams stared at Rhinehart. "You got it all."

Hawkman shot a look at the detective. "Damn! So, that's why Jamey didn't mind giving up part of the diamonds."

CHAPTER THIRTY

Hawkman and Williams left the jewelry store and headed for the police station. The detective pulled up alongside the 4X4 in the visitor's lot and Hawkman hopped out. Before closing the door, he poked his head back inside.

"You know we've been played with hard. She's had plenty of time to get out of the country with hours to spare."

Williams slammed his fist on the steering wheel. "It's not our fault. If the jewelry companies had sent the information out sooner, we might have had a chance to nab her."

"You're right." He shut the door and waved. "I'll talk to you later."

Hawkman went to his office and called the airlines to inquire if all out of country flights had left on time. They had. He dropped the receiver back on the cradle and pulled the passenger list from his inside pocket. Even though he figured it futile, his curiosity made him look through the names. With the initials A.M. in mind, he found the name Amelia Mallory on a flight out of Medford and another on a flight to Cancun out of Los Angeles.

He leaned back in his chair and stared into space.

Jamey hurried down the corridor leading into the Los Angeles terminal and headed for the gate to her next flight. She felt the sweat beading on her forehead and down the center of her back. Even though she figured she'd gotten out of Medford in plenty of time, she feared her plan might have been discovered. The several hours wait for the plane to Cancun had her fidgeting and glancing around the terminal. Hawkman kept looming into her mind. He worried her the most because he had her almost figured to the tee. This made her nervous and she kept her eyes peeled for any sign of a tall man wearing a leather cowboy hat. However, it gave her pleasure to think she'd possibly outwitted one of the smartest investigators around.

The time finally came for her to board and go through the x-ray machine. It made her anxious each time she had to place that bag on the table. She figured by now that the jewelry companies had sent out notices to the airlines about the larger stolen gems. But to her relief, she cleared the checkpoints again and was soon nestled in the airplane's seat. The rumble and vibration of the plane sounded like music to her ears as it taxied down the runway. When the big machine lifted into the air, she felt relief and giddiness within her chest and glanced out the window. In her mind, she waved goodbye to Los Angeles and greeted Cancun, Mexico. She'd soon be out of the country and united with her lover. That is, if he'd been able to get away. She'd e-mailed him that she had to leave immediately or take the risk of discovery. No response had been forthcoming. But tickets for Amelia Mallory awaited at the airline desk, so he'd recognized the urgency of her post. My, how she'd missed him. She'd be so happy when he took over, so she could relax. Once the gems were out of their hands, they'd have plenty of money to live a life of luxury.

Pushing back her seat, she closed her eyes. The next thing she knew the airline attendant shook her shoulder telling her to put up her seat and fasten her seat belt. Jamey glanced out the window to see miles of blue water with a strip of land popping up in the distance. A thrill surged through her.

When she disembarked, she searched the waiting crowd and her heart fell. No where in sight did she see Bob. She slowly made her way toward the center of the terminal. Suddenly, her heart lurched when someone placed a hand on her shoulder.

"Amelia?"

She whirled around and before she could throw her arms around his neck, he caught her wrist and whispered.

"There's a possibility we're being watched. Act as if I'm your boss."

Quickly gaining her composure, she put her hand to her chest. "Oh, Mr. Davenport, I thought you'd forgotten me."

"Not at all, just running late as usual." He took her by the elbow and guided her toward the door. "I have a car waiting out front."

Inside the vehicle, Bob Evans grinned, then reached across the seat and ran his hand up her thigh. "You look and feel absolutely wonderful. I can hardly wait to get you to the hotel."

She looked around nervously. "Who do you think might have been watching us?"

He started the car and drove away from the curb. "The insurance company. They haven't let me rest; grilled me from morning to night, seven days a week. Just within the last few days have they left me alone. I think they finally believed my story. However, we can't be too careful until we get to Buenas Aires." He glanced at her. "You've got the gems?"

She smiled and fingered the ruby around her neck. "Every one of them."

"That's my girl. I have a buyer lined up."

"Oh, by the way. How's your jaw?," she asked.

"I'm doing fine now, but that Hopkins guy had a fist like a rock."

"He used brass knuckles," she smirked.

He shot her a look. "Shit, no wonder I had such pain."

When they reached the hotel room, Bob ordered champagne. Once the sparkling beverage arrived and they were alone, Jamey presented him with the magnificent jewels. After they toasted their success with entwined arms, Bob tucked the gems away, and directed his full attention to her. He pulled off her dark wig, letting her hair cascade onto her shoulders. His eyes glistened. "God, you're beautiful," he said, enfolding her in his arms. Slowly, he removed each article of her clothing, tantalizing her with his tongue as he went. Her breathing heavy with lust, she fumbled with his shirt buttons and pant zipper. Once they were both undressed, he carried her to the bed.

Later, as they lay in each other's arms, Bob fingered the bracelet on her wrist, then sat up and studied it closely. "Jamey, where the hell did you get this?"

"I've always wanted a real diamond bracelet, so I exchanged the zirconias for real ones." She gave him a flirtation smile. "You just might call this my dirty diamond bracelet."

He laughed and flopped back on the pillow. "Damn, woman. You took quite a risk."

"That's why I had to get out of there. Once I'd planted the diamonds in Carl's truck, I knew any jeweler would discover the fake ones real fast."

He looked at her with a solemn expression. "What if I hadn't been able to join you?"

She grinned mischievously. "Oh, I'd have managed here in Cancun. I like beaches, lovely hotels and handsome men."

He pulled her to him. "I have no doubt you'd have done just fine."

❧

After Hawkman zeroed in on Amelia Mallory as being Jamey and tracked the name to a flight going to Cancun, Mexico, his search ended. No way would they be able to get the passenger list of outgoing flights from Cancun unless they had the time, money and man power to pursue the chase. Hawkman doubted it worth the effort and figured the insurance company wouldn't pay for the investigation either. The end payment would cost as much as the jewels, so they might as well settle the claim and put it behind them.

He didn't hurry to give Williams the news of his discovery, as it really wouldn't make much difference on the detective's end. He'd still have to keep the case open as no proof had passed across his desk that Jamey Schyler-Gray was dead or alive.

At the end of the day, Hawkman stopped by the police station and strolled into the detective's office. Williams had his head bowed over a stack of paper work.

"I see they can't keep a guy from doing what he likes best," Hawkman chuckled.

Williams glanced up and tossed his pen on the desk. "Like hell they can't. Sit down and tell me what's on your mind."

Hawkman told him what he'd found out. "I guess about the only thing we can do is turn over the information about Jamey Schyler-Gray, aka Amelia Mallory to the insurance and jewelry companies."

The detective nodded. "Yeah, I'll write up a report and put it on file."

Hawkman left the station and headed for home. He had that let-down feeling of being defeated by a very slick con-artist. And a woman at that.

"You may have escaped me this time Ms. Jamey Schyler-Gray, but don't you ever show your pretty little face in my town again," he said aloud.

He pulled a toothpick from his pocket and stuck it into his mouth. A cigarette would taste mighty good right now.

THE END